THREE OF HEARTS
EROTIC ROMANCE FOR WOMEN

T0056864

Edited by
Kristina Wright

Foreword by Alison Tyler

PRESS

Published in the United States by Cleis Press, an imprint of Start Midnight, LLC, 375 Hudson Street, Twelfth Floor, New York, New York 10014.

Printed in the United States.
Cover design: Scott Idleman/Blink
Cover photograph: Igor Demchenkov/Getty Images
Text design: Frank Wiedemann

First Edition.
10 9 8 7 6 5 4 3 2 1

Trade paper ISBN: 978-1-940550-03-9
E-book ISBN: 978-1-940550-09-1

Contents

FOREWORD:
TRIO, TRIAD,
TRY ONE...

So you want to try a threesome?

Oh, wait. I'm not propositioning you. Don't tilt your head at me like that! I'm simply making the query. You crave the thrill of being with your partner plus a brand-new lover—or of being the third point in another couple's Valentine heart. Well, of course you do.

Two plus one equals three times the emotion, the excitement and the romance. A third can enhance the connection between two lovers in such a dreamy way. Everything that is arousing one-on-one becomes magnified when you add a third. Your hushed whispers now have an audience. There is added potential for being a voyeur, an exhibitionist, a star of the show. Even holding hands becomes a sublime treat when there is an extra player in the mix. And kissing—let's stop and talk about kissing. Who to kiss first? How long to devote to one set of lips? Spin the bottle isn't out of the question when you have three!

The authors in *Three of Hearts* bring desire to the table

in triplicate. From Cheyenne Blue's sultry "What Happens in Denver" to Annabeth Leong's seductive "Whose Anniversary Is It, Anyway?" to editor Kristina Wright's own sizzling "Three for the Road," the stories will wrap you in their trio of silken strands and leave you breathless and aroused.

Consider using these pieces as inspiration to step into your own real-life scenario. Find your favorite and purr the piece to your partner, highlighting exactly how far you'd like to go. Or leave the fantasies on the page, making *Three of Hearts* the third in your relationship. Even if you relegate the scenes to fantasy-only fodder, this collection is designed to take you to the brink.

Another man? Another woman? Another heart to embrace. These stories allow you to pull back the sheets on *both* sides of the bed while you climb in the middle.

Go on. Shuffle that deck. Deal in a third.

XXX,
Alison Tyler
Editor of *Three-Way: Erotic Adventures*

INTRODUCTION: THREE'S THE CHARM

We have all heard the saying that two is company and three is a crowd—but that isn't true for everyone. For adventurous, libidinous souls, three is a magical number with endless possibilities for love and lust to combine and entwine...and be divine! Where two signifies a balance of heart and mind, the number three represents a different kind of relationship, one that is more open to the possibilities, more flexible in its fluidity, more experimental in its sexuality. The number three is a powerful number in mythology and religion, often signifying a completion or wholeness. The modern day digital version of a heart (or love) is created by typing the less than symbol, followed by the number three: <3. What's on the other side of that less than symbol doesn't really matter, you could simply say that when it comes to love, anything is less than three. Put another way: how can you argue that a trio of hearts and libidos finding a balance together is anything less than a grand and amazing thing?

Three of Hearts: Erotic Romance for Women isn't about the joy of a sexy ménage à trois. Okay, it's not *just* about that. There are certainly erotic threesomes to be found here—stories with two of the three being madly in love and wondering what it would be like to bring a third person into their bed, for a one-time experience or a lifetime of lust. But there are also stories here about three people in love. When three people fall for each other, there is a newfound symmetry and balance to the number three. When two of the three are in love with the third person and find a way to share their lives (and bed) with each other, there is a collaboration of desires. When there is conflict between two, there is a third to mediate. When there is joy, it is tripled.

This is a collection of stories about threeways, triads, long-term commitments and one-night stands with the promise of more. Three people sharing their bodies, their fantasies and their futures; three people testing their limits together, emotionally and sexually; three people finding all the possibilities to be had when three *isn't* a crowd at all, it is a fantasy—and lives—fulfilled. Three is magic, three is mysterious, three is a heart turned sideways, looking at life a little differently from the rest.

If three is your lucky number, *Three of Hearts* will delight you with its stories. And if you've never considered the possibilities to be had with two partners, *Three of Hearts* will inspire your wildest fantasies of what could be...with three.

Kristina Wright
In love in Virginia

MOVIE NIGHT

Tiffany Reisz

The argument started the moment the movie ended.

"Not buying it," Leigh said, standing to stretch her legs.

"What aren't you buying?" Her husband Bryce caressed the back of her calf as she picked up the wine bottle and three empty glasses.

"You didn't like the movie? It's a classic thriller." Ethan took the empty bottle and glasses from her and carried them to the bar.

"It was a good movie," Leigh said. "Good acting. Good script. Huge, gaping plot hole you could drive a dump truck through."

Ethan arched an eyebrow at her as he leaned back against the bar. Her husband's best friend since college, Ethan was a regular fixture in their lives. He'd been the best man in their wedding and had suffered good-naturedly through more than a dozen of her attempts to fix him up with friends of hers. She hated playing matchmaker, but anytime her single friends got a look at the six-foot-tall former professional soccer player, they begged for an introduction.

"What's the huge, gaping plot hole?" Bryce asked as his hand slid farther up the back of her dress. She gave him a playful dirty look. Her black-haired, blue-eyed, too-handsome-for-his-own-good husband hit on her constantly when Ethan hung out with them: Bryce's not-so-subtle way of saying, *Look how fun being married is. Aren't you sad you're still single?*

Leigh swatted at his hand. "So the one guy convinces the other guy that they can swap wives in the night, right? 'Here, we'll sneak into each other's houses and while our wives are asleep, we'll initiate sex. And in the dark with them barely awake, they won't realize it's not their husbands fucking them.' That's the plot point, right?" Leigh asked.

"What? We have sex all the time when one or both of us is barely awake," Bryce said, pulling Leigh down onto his lap. "We did last night."

Ethan rolled his eyes, and Leigh winked at him.

"True," she said, remembering waking up with Bryce's erection pressing against her back. She'd pushed back against him, and he'd slid inside her. Without even exchanging a single word, they'd fucked for a few minutes before Bryce pulled out of her and fell back asleep. She'd followed him into dreamland only seconds later. "But I knew it was you, obviously. If it had been some other man in the dark, I would have known. That's the plot hole. A woman would know if the man fucking her is or is not her husband even in the dark and half-asleep. That husband should have known he was getting played by his neighbor." Leigh got off Bryce's lap. She took the DVD out of the player and turned off the television.

"You only say that because you know I'm the only man who's going to be fucking you in the middle of the night. If it was some other guy in our bed, and you were sleepy enough, you wouldn't be able to tell him from me."

"Oh, I could tell," Leigh said, crossing her arms over her chest. "Trust me."

"My cock *is* pretty amazing," Bryce said with a humble sigh. "I guess you're right."

"I think it could work," Ethan said, coming back to the sitting area holding a glass of wine. "You'd have to even the playing field though. No talking, no touching, just cock-in-pussy. And total darkness, of course."

"He's got a point, babe. You know it's me because of my voice and how I touch you." He took Leigh by the wrist and pulled her back down onto his lap. "If you were blindfolded or something and two different guys fucked you without a word, you wouldn't be able to tell the difference."

"I could tell," she said. "And I can prove it."

"How?" Ethan asked, raising the wineglass to his lips.

"Just like Bryce said—blindfold me, don't make noise, and fuck me." She looked at her husband who only laughed a little.

Ethan lowered the wineglass before he'd even taken a drink.

"You mean now?" Ethan asked.

"Why not?" Bryce ran his hand from Leigh's ankle to her hip. "She dissed your favorite movie. You don't want to prove her wrong?"

"Dude, she's your wife."

"You didn't tell him?" Leigh asked.

"I thought he knew," Bryce said.

"Thought I knew what?" Ethan asked.

"Oh, we're kinky as fuck, Ethan," Leigh said.

"I knew he was. I didn't know you were," Ethan said to Leigh.

"We have threesomes at least once a month," Leigh explained

as Bryce kissed her under her ear. "Usually it's me and one of my girlfriends with him, but sometimes it's another guy. I'm never blindfolded though, and I always know who's fucking me. This could be interesting."

"Want to?" Bryce looked up at Ethan.

"Do I want to fuck your wife?" Ethan looked at Bryce and then back at her. "You don't even have to ask."

"I'll get the stuff," Leigh said, scrambling off Bryce's lap. "Are we in here or the bedroom? Preference, Ethan?"

He still wore a look of *Did I just win the lottery?* "In here, I guess. I think I'd feel even weirder doing this in your bedroom," Ethan said.

"Suit yourself," Leigh said and headed to the bedroom. She opened the trunk under the window and found the heaviest of their blindfolds. From the nightstand, she grabbed a box of condoms and the bottle of lubricant. In front of the mirror she paused long enough to tuck a stray tendril of red hair back into place and to adjust the straps of her pale-yellow sundress she'd been running around in all day. Ethan always said he wouldn't get married until he found a redhead as sweet as her. Why should Bryce have all the luck? Leigh shimmied out of her panties and left them on the bedroom floor. Oh, Ethan. A wide grin spread across Leigh's face. Would he still think she was "sweet" after tonight?

She returned to the den where Bryce and Ethan had already moved the coffee table out of the way. Bryce laid a blanket on the floor over the Oriental rug. They'd learned the hard way not to fuck on that rug without something between her back and the rough pile.

"Put on some music," Bryce said to her. "It'll mask any stray sounds."

"I don't know if our speakers can get loud enough to mask

your breathing, darling," Leigh said as she queued up some instrumental blues on her stereo.

"I get loud," Bryce said to Ethan, who only laughed. "But I can keep it quiet tonight. It's just part of the challenge."

"Here. Take this." Leigh gave the blindfold to Ethan. "Can you tie it on me?"

"Yeah, of course. Are you sure about this?" he asked as she turned her back to him. He placed the blindfold, a thick black sash, over her eyes and tied it with a firm knot. The world went dark. She saw nothing at all, not even a sliver of light from above or below the blindfold.

"Bryce?" she asked.

"Go for it, babe."

Leigh reached behind her and found Ethan's hands. She pulled them around her body and placed them on her breasts. She heard Ethan's breath catch in his throat. With the blindfold covering her eyes, her other senses heightened, grew more acute. She felt Ethan's heart pounding as she pressed her back into his chest.

"Touch me anywhere," she whispered. "Bryce likes to watch."

She shivered as she felt Ethan's lips on her shoulder. He squeezed her breasts gently. The heat of his hands through the cotton caused her nipples to harden against his palms.

"Don't be nervous," she said as she took his right wrist in her hand and guided him lower. "I've wanted this with you for a long time. I even told Bryce."

"You did?" Ethan whispered back as he slid his hand under her dress.

She spread her legs and leaned back farther into him. Ethan slid his hand between her thighs and carefully caressed her clitoris.

"I did," she said as she pushed her hips against his hand. "He's fucked a few of my friends. It's only fair I get one of his."

"Only fair," Ethan agreed, pushing a finger into her. Leigh turned her head up and back and Ethan kissed her. Their mouths met, their tongues mingled, and all the while he fucked her with his finger. "You wouldn't believe how many times you've been in my fantasies." Ethan pushed a second finger into her wetness.

"Oh, I can believe it," she teased.

"Shall we?" Bryce's voice cut through the darkness and the haze of her desire.

"Definitely," she whispered against Ethan's lips.

She felt Bryce's hands on her waist as he guided her a few steps forward to the end of the blanket. Carefully he brought her down to the floor. She stretched out on her back. Bryce gave her the tube of lubricant. She raised her dress to her waist and spread a thin layer of lube over her vulva.

"You both are just standing there watching me do this, aren't you?" she asked.

"Of course not," Bryce said.

"We totally are," Ethan said.

"Thought so." Leigh closed the bottle and set it aside. Her heart raced in anticipation.

"We should make this game a little more interesting," Bryce said as Leigh opened her legs even wider.

"How so?" she asked.

"If Leigh can tell who's fucking her, she picks the next movie. If she guesses wrong, we do. For the next year."

"Sounds fair," Leigh said. "Hope you boys like old Hollywood musicals."

"I hate musicals, dude. We have *got* to win this game," Ethan said.

The room went silent but for the sound of the music playing

in the background. Leigh strained her ears to hear any hints about what was happening in the room.

She sensed someone kneeling between her thighs and heard the metal jingling of a belt buckle opening. Then she heard the foil of a condom package ripping. With each little sound she grew more and more aroused, more and more nervous. She really wanted to win this damn game.

The tip of a cock started to nudge against her vaginal lips. She reached down, spread her folds, and sighed as someone entered her in one smooth, slow stroke. The thrust was sure and steady. Must be Bryce then. Ethan would be more tentative as they'd never even kissed before tonight, much less fucked.

Yes, she knew these thrusts...long, heavy, steady thrusts. Her husband's thrusts—loving, possessive...rough and tender at the same time. Usually by now he'd have one of her breasts in his mouth and her clitoris between his fingers as he brought her to orgasm again and again. But the rules were already set—just penis in vagina and thrusting. She had to know the man by the feel and movement of his cock in her alone.

After a few minutes with the first man inside her, Leigh started to ache for an orgasm. But instead, the man pulled out of her. She sensed him moving away from her.

"Want to take a guess?" came Bryce's voice. "Was that me or Ethan?"

"I think I need a comparison," she said. "Just to be sure I can tell the difference."

Bryce laughed, and she grinned at the ceiling and thanked god for giving her a husband as sexually adventurous as she was.

Once more she sensed a presence between her thighs, once more she heard pants opening, foil ripping. The floor creaked. Leigh sensed hands on either side of her shoulders. Again someone entered her—more carefully this time. She moaned at the pleasure of the penetration as either Ethan or Bryce, she didn't care who as long as he didn't stop, started slamming his hips into hers. She grabbed her legs behind the knees and held herself open wider. Bryce had fucked her like this many times— hard, fast, ramming into her like he'd die if he didn't fuck her into the ground in the next five minutes. But it could have been Ethan. He'd confessed just minutes ago that she'd been in many of his sexual fantasies. Perhaps this was him, his pent-up longing for her manifesting in this brutal pounding.

She gasped in surprise as she felt another presence right next to her.

"Can you tell yet?" came Bryce's breathless voice.

"Is it me or Bryce?" Ethan asked, his voice equally strained.

"Maybe she needs more to go on," Bryce said.

Leigh shivered as fingers slipped up her arm and pulled the strap of her sundress down her left arm and then her right. A few loosened buttons later and her bare breasts spilled out of her dress. A mouth, hot and hungry, latched on to her left nipple. But if that mouth belonged to the man inside her, she couldn't tell.

Another mouth found her right nipple and sucked it hard. She arched up off the floor as pleasure coursed from her breasts to a spot deep inside her hips. Still the cock inside worked her to a wet frenzy. She could feel her own fluid leaking out and onto the blanket beneath her.

A hand slid between her stomach and the male stomach above her. Two fingers found her swollen clitoris and teased it. The teasing turned to torture as those same fingers pinched and tugged it gently as the thrusts into her turned from fast and frenzied to long, deep strokes that she felt all the way against her cervix.

"Who is it, babe?" Bryce taunted, his voice seeming to come from over her and next to her at the same time. "Who is fucking you right now?"

"You both are," she said knowing the cock inside her didn't belong to the fingers on her clitoris.

"Not quite..." her husband whispered. "But it's the best idea I've heard all night."

The man inside her, Ethan or Bryce, pulled out of her. Someone pushed her onto her side.

"You know what to do, Leigh," Bryce said, his voice quiet and commanding. She loved him most in his dominant moods when he took control of her body and used it like his own personal sex toy. She did know what to do. She and her husband had anal sex at least once a week. While lying on her side, she pulled her knees up to her chest as Bryce worked his lube-covered fingers into her, opening her up enough to take him inside her.

As she lay in position, she heard movement, footsteps, and men changing position. Did this mean it was Ethan who now spooned up against her and started to push into her ass? Or was it a trick and once more was it Bryce behind her? Inch by inch, whoever it was pushed into her as her body strained to accommodate him. Once inside her, the man wrapped an arm over her chest and rolled them both onto their backs. Hands grasped her breasts and pulled her nipples. Someone took her knees in his hands and shoved them wide. Again the kneeling and the penetration. Leigh shuddered as the second cock entered her, this time shoving itself deep into her vagina.

Mute with ecstasy, Leigh could only breathe as the two men worked in tandem, fucking her with hard but careful thrusts. She'd experienced double penetration before. Bryce often put a vibrator in her vagina while he fucked her ass, but never before had she had two men in her at the same time. She'd never felt so filled before, filled almost to bursting. She felt everything, every nerve fired, every muscle tightened and contracted and stretched to take them both.

Fingers found her clitoris again and teased it. She came hard, jerking in the arms that held her. But the men, neither of them, were done with her. They continued to thrust into her. Each inward thrust left her gasping. Each time they pulled out, she moaned. Her hands grasped at the shoulders above her as the chest beneath her back rose and fell and rose again.

It was too much. Sensation overwhelmed her. She came a second time and the cry that escaped her lips sounded pained even to her. The man in her pussy pulled out. The man beneath her rolled her back onto her side and slid out of her as well.

She thought they'd finished with her but two hands grabbed her hips and brought her up onto her hands and knees. She heard more foil ripping and in seconds the cock entered her vagina again from behind. Limp from her two orgasms, Leigh could do nothing but take it as the cock slammed into her. Hands gathered her breasts and held them as the man inside her rode out his own orgasm with a few final, brutal thrusts.

Once more she was moved. This time she was made to straddle someone's hips. She placed her hands on his chest to steady herself while his penis slid between her wet lips and pressed into her. The two hands on her hips ground her against the hips beneath her. When she felt a presence standing before her, she raised her hands. She felt the smooth skin of a flat male stomach under her palms as the cock pushed between her lips.

It nudged her throat and she opened her mouth even wider to receive it. One hand cradled the back of her neck. Fingers brushed against her cheek. If her mouth hadn't been otherwise occupied, she would have smiled.

She rocked her hips harder against the man beneath her. His

hands dug into her skin as he worked her on his cock until he pushed up and into her with one final thrust before going still under her. The cock in her mouth pumped a few more times before she tasted semen, warm and salty, inside her mouth. He pulled out, and she swallowed.

Four hands put her onto her back. She tugged her dress up and buttoned the front. She smoothed her skirt down and rolled into a sitting position.

"I guess we win, Ethan," Bryce said.

Leigh reached up behind her head and untied the blindfold.

"It was you first, Bryce," she said. "Then Ethan. Then Ethan again. You were in my ass, Bryce, while Ethan fucked my pussy. Bryce finished off while I was on my hands and knees. Ethan was under me while I was on top. It was your cock, my handsome husband, that was just in my mouth."

She raised her hand and wiped off her wet lips. Bryce and Ethan, both sitting side by side on the couch, looked at each other and then at her.

"If you knew, why didn't you guess?" Ethan asked.

"I didn't want to win too soon." She grinned at them both. "Then you might have stopped."

"How did you know?" Bryce asked.

"I knew it was you the first time," Leigh said, "because I could smell your soap. I buy the soap so of course I knew it was you. When you were in my mouth, I could feel your wedding ring when you touched my face. The rest were educated guesses. Was I right?"

Ethan nodded. "You got it. I guess we're stuck watching fucking musicals for the next year," he sighed, then smiled at Bryce.

"I hate musicals." He dropped his head back and Leigh only laughed at her poor tortured husband.

"Well, how about this idea…?" Leigh asked as she crawled across the floor and rested her head in Bryce's lap. She reached out and took Ethan's hand in hers.

"What?" Bryce prompted.

She looked up at her husband and smiled.

"Next time we have movie night, we just skip the movie."

AN EXTRA
PAIR OF EYES

Rachel Kramer Bussel

B illie could have tried to pretend she was putting an extra
coat of lip gloss on for Clyde's sake, but the smile dancing
upon her now super-shiny lips wasn't for her husband. Or
rather, it wasn't for her husband alone. Nor was the tug of
desire echoing from deep within her. She knew the difference
after four years together. There were times when she wanted
nothing more than to rip Clyde's clothes off, or he came home
and barely said hello before he was lifting her onto the nearest
piece of furniture and kissing her so passionately she lost any
thoughts in her head.

But there were other times when what lit her up, inside and
out, was the thrill of checking out someone new, imagining his
or her lips pressed against hers. Or, in this case, pressed against
hers and Clyde's. She didn't know whether Mr. Ripped Jeans
and Sexy Stubble would be into that, but the high of flirting
with a stranger was that she didn't need to know. Simply giving
him the Look was enough to make her heart pound so hard she

had to force herself to take a deep breath, lest she lose her head entirely.

That breath didn't help when she returned to the bar and the guy patted the stool next to him. He'd already ordered her a drink, one clearly far stronger than her planned Diet Coke. Clyde was running late, so why not? She smiled, pursing her glossy lips. "Well, thank you. Dare I ask what this is?"

"Why don't you guess?" His voice made her grip the edge of the bar and tighten the press of her thighs against each other. The tight seam of her jeans taunted her as she shifted, bending low to sip from the edge of the martini glass. She avoided looking at him just then, sure her pale face was by now hot pink.

"A cosmo? Really? That's the best you could do?" She couldn't help the complaint, even as the heat from the sweet drink made its way through her body.

The stranger gave her a good long look up and down. "What did you have in mind instead, princess?"

"First, it's princess types who drink cosmos—not me. Second, I'll take a Maker's Mark. Neat. I'm Billie."

"My treat," he said, the words warming her far more than her generous sip had. She tapped her fingers on the wood, grateful she'd been growing out her nails and had just gotten them painted in her favorite red, the manicure equivalent of fuck-me heels.

As Billie sank into a fantasy about just how many ways this stranger could heat her—and Clyde—up, in the back of her mind, she knew she'd have to convince her husband. It's not that he wasn't adventurous in bed—he was up for almost anything— but he had his pride, and it was no secret that a threesome pushed some touchy buttons for him. Whenever the topic had come up before, Clyde had made it clear he was afraid that what Billie really wanted was a man with a bigger cock, a rougher touch—in other words, a man who wasn't him. No matter how many ways she'd reassured him that she didn't want someone to replace him and never would, her explanations never quite got through to him.

At first, she'd been embarrassed and uncertain; maybe she was asking for too much, being too greedy. But the more she thought about it, the surer she was that Clyde would actually like it if there were another man in the room with them. She knew him well enough to know he'd get off on an extra pair of eyes to ogle him when she played with his nipples or tapped the riding crop against his balls or teasingly licked her way up his shaft, an extra pair of hands to hold Clyde open as she pressed a plug right against his hole before sinking it deep inside, and an extra set of lips to kiss Clyde's when she was busy. Every time they'd done something as remotely risqué as getting handsy in a movie theater, or she'd mentioned someone checking him out, Clyde had reacted. Maybe he didn't realize that his breathing got heavier, his cock harder, but she did. She'd bet good money that once in an intimate setting with her and another man—or another woman—Clyde would happily enjoy triple the pleasure.

Perhaps all that sounded selfless, when in fact she was being selfish. The very idea of watching another man enjoy her husband in the way she did made her mad with lust. Yet up until then, it had been just that for her—an idea, a fantasy, a utopian dream. She'd let herself succumb to Clyde's doubts, despite every part of her tingling with anticipation when she pictured in flagrant detail what the three of them could get up to.

"For you," Mr. Cosmo said, presenting her a new glass with a flourish, a look of amusement and arousal on his face. This sexy stranger seemed like he might just be the answer to her dreams. The more they communicated, silently and through words, the more her entire body heated up. He had the one quality every man she'd ever bedded had shared: the ability to look at her like he could see every dirty thought percolating in her mind. In turn, that knowingness made her want to share all her extremely dirty—filthy, really—thoughts. And just as she drained her last sip of what had turned out to be a very delicious cosmo, Billie leaned over and went for it. After all, if you can't tell a stranger who buys you a drink and looks at you like you're naked what you're really thinking, why bother? "I'm married. But I still want to take you home with me. With us. As a treat. Like a Christmas present in...April. You'd be a gift to my husband, Clyde. But I'd get to unwrap you."

Billie made sure her lips touched the man's ear, an ear she was suddenly very hungry to nibble on, to run her tongue along the delicate skin, to see what would happen when she made contact. She wanted to look down at the ground, to let her blush say everything she couldn't, after that confession, but she used her liquid courage to stare right up into those mesmerizing blue eyes. She stared steadily, directly, not wanting to pretend she hadn't just dropped a bomb on him, albeit, she hoped, a sexy bomb. Her eyes didn't beg or promise; they simply looked, absorbing him, giving him a teaser of what she would look like naked, raw, stripped totally bare.

"You want to play with me, is what you're asking, Billie? You and Clyde?" He drew out the words, his gaze jumping from her eyes very deliberately to her lips, moving almost imperceptibly closer as he dangled the promise of his presence before her.

"Yes. I want to watch you two...and touch you two. I want you to fuck Clyde. And fuck me." She hadn't planned to say the F word once, let alone twice. It sounded so dirty out in the open like that, and yet it was the only word that would get across exactly what she wanted. She wanted to see this man's cock, to take it in her hands, to wrap her lips around it, to watch it enter her husband, and later, to feel it impale her. She wanted it all, but asking a total stranger to give it to her was an experience Billie hadn't indulged in for longer than she could remember.

He tugged her stool closer to his, the air between them now utterly electrified. She felt drunk from the intensity of his stare, from the way he'd taken her favorite fantasy and suddenly made it all too real. "And what do I get in return, Billie, for fucking both of you?"

The question was one only a man utterly confident in himself could ask. What would he get in return? Anything he wanted. But she couldn't say that. She couldn't give away the small semblance of control she still possessed. "What do you want?" she asked.

"I want you to take both of us at the same time. If your husband is even a tenth as hot as you are, I'm sure he'll be a delight to play with, but you seem like the kind of woman who could probably easily take three cocks and just barely be satisfied. I guess two will have to do tonight."

If she'd thought his buying her a drink was presumptuous, what he'd just said was beyond, well, cocky, but it did its job. She was so turned on she could barely reply, picturing, in that moment, the luxury of having three hard cocks to enjoy simultaneously. "You want to touch me right now, don't you?" he asked. They were starting to go afoul of the rules she'd made with Clyde, the ones that allowed her to flirt, but not touch, as well as requiring her to report to Clyde any man she was flirting with. He'd get to witness her getting her flirt on soon enough, right? She certainly didn't want to feed his paranoia about her being on the hunt for someone better. And yet, the tingling not just between her legs but up and down the length of her body, and the awareness of exactly how turned on this man was making her, was undeniable.

"I do," she said, struggling to keep her voice steady. She inched slightly closer, smiling to herself with the knowledge that in her younger, single days, she'd already have been in this man's lap. But she didn't truly want to be—not yet. She liked the restraint, the courtesy, the anticipation. Billie liked having rules to bind her, just as surely as she liked to be bound with rope or cuffs or commands. The rules didn't take away any of the hotness—they added to it. "But I have to wait. For Clyde. That's the rule."

He raised an eyebrow, as if to suggest rules were made to be broken. That was true, but it only worked if it was a rule you truly wanted to break. Billie wanted the rules, and she wanted her way, her fantasy come to life. And just like that, she knew she was going to get it. "I may look like they're not my thing, but I actually like rules. The right ones, anyway." She batted her lashes to make the words less of a rejection. She could see his hardness straining against his jeans, and that one quick look made her want to look again.

"So what should we do while we wait, Billie?" He sat back, leaving her suddenly lonely without his breath landing on her skin.

She forced herself not to bite her lip or look down or start to nibble on a fingernail. "We could talk." She let the last word dangle between them, having spoken it as if it were as filthy as *fuck*. The bartender seamlessly slipped her a new glass of whiskey in place of the one she'd downed. Billie wanted to keep her wits about her, but she needed something to do with her mouth that didn't involve this stranger's skin, so she picked it up.

"Cheers," he said, holding up his glass to clink with hers.

"Cheers," she replied. The single syllable was fraught with

tension. She could be drinking water and she was sure it would burn in the same delicious way. The heat came from something else entirely—the prospect of bedding this man, and her man. Billie was quite clear on the distinction, which made it all the more thrilling—she didn't want two men to call her own, a husband and a lover, or even a plaything, on the side. She wanted Clyde, and the thrill of six hands seeking and searching and finding each other. She wanted this hunk of a human to do things to Clyde that she, not even with the world's most advanced sex toys, couldn't do. She wanted to watch—and to participate. The more she drank, the more she realized she couldn't convey to Clyde in words what it was she craved. No words would ever be quite enough to assuage his fears. But seeing, she was convinced, would beget believing, and he knew what she looked like when she was utterly turned on. All she had to do was get them to kiss—for a start—and Clyde would surely see where this could lead.

She paced herself with the drink, letting the man run his hands along her legs, her arms, through her hair. She'd told Clyde when to show up, before she'd somehow managed to conjure up this delightful specimen of manhood beside her, but her husband was never a stickler for punctuality, so she wasn't holding her breath. Especially not when the now not-such-a-stranger said things like, "I bet you look amazing when you come." How does one answer such a compliment without sounding utterly narcissistic or else insincere? She just laughed—hoping he'd find out.

She liked the tension building between them. When she'd been single, she'd rarely stopped to savor tension—it was *attention* she wanted, that was the prize, even more than getting naked with someone else. Once she had a man eating out of the palm of her hand—sometimes literally—Billie was always the one who lost interest, the tension vanishing along with the chase. This was different. The tension crackled between them, growing, building, changing as they shifted positions, bantered, waited. Again, she smiled to herself, though he could surely see her lips move; it hit her like a lightning bolt that she could savor the tension, however long it lasted, because her own relationship was solid and secure, a sure thing. She could never savor the sexual tension when she felt she had to impress someone with every aspect of her personality; there was always something he could find wanting after their bedroom antics were done.

She was so lost in that tension when Clyde finally arrived, he took her by surprise. Her breath caught as she looked down at him towering over the two of them, took in his scent—she'd never known pure clean soap could smell so sexy. "Hello there," he said smoothly, pulling a stool up to form a triangle of bodies. "I'm Clyde," he added casually, sticking out his left hand while placing his right one on her shoulder.

"Tate." So that was his name—one she certainly wouldn't forget. Funny that she hadn't asked in all their time chatting and drinking. The lone syllable hung in the air. Where some guys might have tossed it out as challenge along with their hand-shake, she could tell from the way he carried himself that Tate wasn't threatened by Clyde. They hadn't exactly had a heart-to-heart, but she'd made it clear Clyde was part of her package deal.

She slid slightly closer to Tate on her stool while keeping Clyde's arm around her. "Thanks for entertaining my wife," Clyde offered.

"Oh, she was the one entertaining me." The tone had shifted from convivial to conspiratorial; somehow Billie, who'd been running the show all afternoon, was now the object of the conversation. All kinds of sparks were zinging back and forth between the men; the cumulative effect made her achingly wet.

"Shall we?" Clyde asked, taking the words right out of her mouth. Somehow, he'd read their body language and gotten it—Clyde knew that he was the center of this trio, the whole reason she wanted to indulge in the first place. By keeping her grounded, he also let her fly, knowing he'd be there to catch her. She wanted both of them—all three of them—to fly now, together. Letting him take the lead would give her a sense of what he was comfortable with.

"Where to?"

"You can follow me. Actually, Billie can go with you. She knows the way. Our usual room," he murmured softly to her. The words sent another blast of arousal through her, along with the implication that this was a regular occurrence for them. Hooking up in hotel rooms was—that they made sure to do at least once a month—but never picking up a stranger. Her flirtatious dabblings had only gone so far as kissing and groping, and had all been with trusted, vetted friends.

She didn't ask if he was sure, worried that any one of them might back out. Sometimes you just had to take a chance, lest you ruin the moment with too much guesswork. Clyde's eyes on her, so full of love and lust, were enough. She followed Tate to his car. As she reached for her seat belt, he put his hand out and stopped her. "Wait," he said, running his hand along her cheek before pulling her close for a long, deep kiss, the kind that would have been utterly inappropriate in the bar, the kind that left her mouth ravenous for more.

They didn't talk on the way; Tate followed Clyde to the tucked-away hotel, one big enough to allow for a semblance of anonymity, but small enough to offer luxury service. They

followed Clyde in; for all her openness, Billie blushed fiercely as
Tate held her left hand and Clyde grabbed her right. There was
no doubt about what she was doing here—fucking two men.
Never mind that one was her husband, the love of her life.

Soon they were in a familiar place, the hotel room she and
Clyde had been renting for over two years, at least once a
month. They'd hit a patch that she wouldn't quite call rough,
but had definitely been a little rocky, where sex took a backseat
to watching TV, where desire seemed like a foreign language
she could only remember a word of here or there. When she'd
stumbled across an ad for the hotel, she'd visited it and booked a
room as a surprise. The change of scenery had kick-started their
sex life back into high gear, and they'd promised each other
that no matter what, they'd make sure to get back at least once
a month.

Billie shook her head and looked at the two men standing
so close to her, each handsome in his own way. The stranger—
Tate, she reminded herself—looked like he belonged in an ad for
men's cologne or cigarettes, something rugged and manly. Clyde
looked like he belonged in an upscale cigar bar, surrounded by
men in suits. He looked like that even at the beach, even naked.
She'd never want to have to choose between them, but having
both of them right now was everything she could've dreamed
of. She was just about to try to get them started on the scenario
she'd spun for Tate earlier when Clyde grabbed her, pulling her
wrists behind her back.

"You don't mind if you lose a few buttons, do you, Billie?"
he asked in a tone she wasn't sure she'd heard before. They'd
engaged in their share of rough sex, spanking and being spanked,
but this was different. Clyde was offering her to Tate in the same
way she'd pretty much offered Clyde's ass to Tate earlier.

"You mean you want me to do this?" Tate asked Clyde, easily

ripping the pearly buttons from her top, then pulling the cups of her bra down so her nipples burst forth, rising toward Tate in greeting. "You're even more beautiful than I thought you'd be," he said. Clyde's hold on her wrists tightened as Tate bent down to take one nipple between his lips, his fingers reaching for the other. She squirmed, more for something to do than because she wanted to actually escape. Clyde stepped closer, so she could feel his chest against her back, his hardness through his pants. Tate sucked each nipple perfectly—hard, but not too hard—until she knew her jeans were damp between her legs.

"Sometimes my wife just can't get enough cock," Clyde said. The words were filthy, and could have had a mean edge, but they didn't. Clyde sounded proud of her, if anything. Where had that come from? "Isn't that right, Billie?" Before she could answer, he went on. "I bet right now she could handle three cocks—maybe even more." How had he managed to harken back to what she and Tate had just discussed?

Billie moaned at the vision that brought to her mind of being surrounded by hard, eager men each wanting a piece of her. "Take off her pants, and I'm sure she'll show you what she can do." Hearing Clyde talk about her like that—like he was in charge of her and knew exactly how big a slut she was—made her ache all over. Clyde got her—whether or not this was really his fantasy, he knew it was hers. He knew she wanted to be used, taken, fucked. Not worshipped, not adored, but flung around while they took their fill. And just then, that was exactly what she wanted. The woman who'd been in charge of her three-some fantasy at the bar, in theory, gave way to the girl who was putty in their hands. Clyde positioned her on the bed so she was leaning on him, her head in his lap while he stroked her face.

Tate pulled off her jeans and wet panties, revealing the smattering of pubic hair she kept because Clyde liked it. Tate did too, apparently, rubbing his hand along her mons, then tugging on her hairs, before sliding a finger deep inside. Clyde's hold tightened on her, one hand reaching for her hair and tugging as Tate pressed into her, his lone finger somehow filling her up in the most wonderful way. She'd pictured Tate filling Clyde up, the men kissing and groping and writhing, their pleasure in turn becoming hers. But she hadn't pictured the two of them ganging up on her, the instant bond of sexual teamwork they'd form.

"Is she ready to get fucked, Tate?" Clyde asked. Billie whimpered, then let out even louder noises as Clyde held her wrists down while Tate added another finger.

"Oh yes, very ready." Tate's fingers appeared before her lips, and she sucked them deep into her mouth.

"You can have a cock in your mouth later, my love," Clyde said. "Right now I have something else in mind for you. Stay here," he ordered her. She obeyed, but couldn't help looking up as the two men crossed the room, whispering. She saw a smile form on Clyde's lips, then watched as Tate pulled him close for a kiss. Clyde hadn't said she couldn't touch herself, and seeing that extremely hot kiss necessitated her finger rubbing her clit. When Tate reached for Clyde's pants and began to undress her husband, she had to pinch her nipples one at a time while mashing her palm hard against her sex, wishing for a vibrator.

The two men took their time getting undressed and making sure their cocks were very, very hard. She let out a moan as Clyde rolled a condom down over Tate's cock. Her ever-handy husband whipped out a small bottle of lube and added some to each of their lengths. "Don't disappointment me after all this buildup, Billie. You've been saying for years that you wanted two cocks at once, so that's what you're getting." Clyde climbed onto the bed and gave her as deep a kiss as Tate had given him, rolling her on top of him and somehow sliding his cock inside her and holding open her asscheeks in quick succession. She got scared for a second and almost told them to go more slowly, but Clyde rescued her. "Take your time, man," he said, as casually as if Tate were pouring a drink rather than about to fuck her ass.

Tate was a gentleman, though, for all his sex appeal, and dove between her cheeks to lick her thoroughly. Having his tongue buried so deep inside her bottom while Clyde filled her pussy was incredible. She kissed Clyde again and breathed deeply as Tate shifted so the head of his cock was at her entrance. Clyde's fingers still dug into her, holding her cheeks wide in invitation. When Tate started to press inside her, Billie let go of every preconceived idea of what a threesome would be like, and simply savored the feeling of being sandwiched between two men, one she loved, one she'd lusted after, all of them intent on each other's pleasure, and their own.

She'd enjoyed Clyde taking her ass many times, but it had always made her pussy feel left out, empty, greedy. With both of them pressing into her, however, she felt complete. Thinking about how close their cocks were to each other inside her made her tremble. "Yeah, that feels so good, baby," Clyde said softly. Tate kissed the back of her neck, and she once again squirmed, happily "trapped" between them. When Tate's arms wrapped around her and Clyde, she smiled, everything inside her fluttering and spinning and melting into oblivion.

"You're so tight, Billie," said Tate, "you're gonna make me come."

"Me too," said Clyde. She'd known they were close, but hearing it made it more real. She was well into her third orgasm when she felt Clyde erupting inside her, followed by Tate's release. She buried her head in Clyde's shoulder for a moment, while he engulfed them all in a triply entwined hug.

After a minute, they slowly separated, the men going to wash up. She lay in peaceful bliss until she heard the shower start up. Billie couldn't resist heading to the bathroom to join them, but when she found them kissing passionately beneath the mist, she was more than content to watch—an extra pair of eyes to add to the sexy spectacle.

EVE'S APPLE RED

Angela Caperton

It started with Coral Pink on his lapel, then Sinful Cinnamon on his shirt collar. Since then, I've seen them all, really, from Candy Rose to Mischief Mauve, Frosted Spice to Licorice Whip. Learning the exact names of lipstick colors had become a sort of hobby for me.

I had also learned to reconcile my jealousies over Sander's fans, but sometimes I couldn't help feeling a green-eyed sting. For twelve years, I'd managed to keep a lid on the occasional unreasonable jolt when I saw lipstick smears on his clothes or face. The Passion Fruit Crème near his fly had been one of those moments, until I saw the special news segment that aired the following day. Relief turned my bones weak as I watched his graceless-but-game attempt to dance with two Las Vegas showgirls complete with feathery headdresses, sequined bikinis, and false lashes tipped in gold. As the music ended, the women slid down Sander's body to kneel, their heads at his waist, the feathers tickling my husband's nose.

I never had any reason to question Sander's loyalty to me. After ten years of marriage and two years of dating before that, we were comfortable. He worked hard and had gained a reputation as an honest, compassionate and insightful man. Good ratings and his charisma led to his own local morning talk show. Sander's visibility and good looks also made him an object of women's, and some men's, starstruck fantasies. Public smooches went along with the fame.

Twelve years of Crimson Blush and Raspberry Swirl and not once had I any serious reason to question him.

Until Eve's Apple Red.

Of course, I didn't know it was Eve in the beginning. The first smudge had been a missed spot on his ear. Sander tried not to torment me with the lipstick, but he wasn't always the best at cleaning the traces of his fans' adorations, so sometimes I found missed smears on his clothes when I took them to the laundry.

A week later, Eve marked the collar on the polo shirt Sander wore while taping a show at the county fair. I didn't know Eve's brand name though, until I saw the traces of that same sly red on the chain to Sander's St. Christopher medal and took time to identify it. Then, when I saw the unmistakable color on his collar three days later, the spike of jealousy that cut through my stomach could have lanced a wild boar.

Two more times that month I saw Eve, which of course begged the question, how many times had I not seen her?

I refused to ask Sander about Eve. How could I when I'd ignored Nutmeg Nights and Sunset Sweet? I knew Eve was different, but Sander seemed the same to me. The smudges couldn't tell me everything, but the few I found felt intimate, maybe even desperate. Okay, perhaps not desperate, but there was no doubt they were more than simple sigh-filled fan delight.

I wasn't naïve and I wasn't an ostrich, but if I was going to hack through the trust Sander and I shared, I needed more than several smudges of rich, creamy red to force my hand. I would be stronger than my jealousy and my suspicion. Until Sander gave me reason, I was going to be a rock—a marble statue of calm resolve.

That lasted until the jack-o'-lantern cutting contest—live on WZDD, Channel 5. I didn't join Sander at the station often, but the contest brought in several of the city's best artists and chefs, the carved pumpkins to be auctioned off for charity. I gladly volunteered to staff the auction phones while I watched my husband in action.

I answered phones and laughed and smiled as Sander interviewed the contestants, cracked jokes, and spoke with sincere concern about the youth facility the auction proceeds would benefit. As kids from the facility carved their own pumpkins, Sander brilliantly balanced the art of the professional competition against the preteens' efforts as they cut crude faces into bright orange flesh. When the show closed, my handsome husband with his sandy-blond hair and slightly crooked nose called the behind-the-scenes folks out to take a bow.

And there she was—Eve's Apple Red—a lithe, tall, older woman, as graceful as a duchess, her shoulder-length black hair pulled back with a tasteful cloisonné barrette, her completely professional skirt and blouse brought to sexy life by a string of pearls that teased the swell of her breasts and dipped just below the V of her low-buttoned shirt.

The auction line rang but I couldn't answer. I could only stare at the woman. She looked at my Sander with such longing, such want, and as Sander's arm closed around her waist in a friendly hug, he looked at her, his face frozen in his star smile, but I also saw his tension, the little pull at the corners of his eyes. When Eve placed a kiss on his cheek, I knew without a doubt, she was the one.

Eve. Executive Producer Marsha Lommex.

When I got home that evening, Sander sat on the sofa, his head back, his eyes closed in light slumber. An empty wineglass sat on the end table, a bleed of burgundy tinting it pink. I pulled the ottoman in front of him and sat, watching him sleep, his face still, but set.

I reached out and stroked his legs, a loving kneading that I wished could somehow pull his thoughts to me, reveal my fears as truths or dispel them entirely. He woke, blinking rapidly, and groggily sitting up.

"Started without you," he said, his smile sheepish as he leaned forward to kiss me.

Would he like Eve's Apple Red on me? I wondered as I gently nipped his lower lip.

"The postgame analysis of the auction took forever, but I think we managed about six thousand dollars for the center."

"That's great!" He stretched and looked over his shoulder at the clock in the wall. "Damn. I should hit the sack. Gotta be in early tomorrow."

The stab of jealousy shocked me with its tearing violence. "Early? Why?"

Why. I hate that word and I hated that it came out of me. Why. It's too close to "whine" and so often they're one and the same.

"Crystal Lake marathon is tomorrow." He leaned forward and kissed my cheek as he rose. I reached out to grip his hands, wordless, and gently pulled him back down onto the sofa.

"It was good to put a face with the color."

Sander looked at me, his brow furrowing. "Color?"

I gave a short chuckle, taking the teasing approach. "Eve's

Apple Red. It's Marsha who keeps kissing you."

Sander grinned, a guilty turn that reminded me of a frat boy caught with his girlfriend's underwear. "She's a sweetheart."

"She likes you."

"Sure she does. She helps finance the show."

"She should help finance your dry cleaning as well." I looked down and said again, "She likes you."

He didn't say anything for the span of a decade, then he said all he needed to. "Yeah."

That single word weighted by acknowledgment also burned with admission. Her affection was not unrequited.

Who wouldn't want a bite of that apple?

"Lisa, isn't it?"

Marsha smiled at me, her lips painted to perfection, the color so deep and precisely applied, a smooth invitation, guile-less and open. I looked into the face of a woman I half wanted to become—composed, elegant, her skirt-suit tailored to a body that was fit, but graceful in showcasing hips above the slightest fluff around her belly. Her waist curved in, her breasts filled a bra that didn't try to push up or enhance her cleavage. I could almost see a hint of lace beneath the translucent blouse. Age had lightly creased the corners of her eyes, and a hint of laugh-lines made pale parentheses to frame her mouth's beauty.

My belly tightened, and I better understood Sander's conflict—I felt it myself with just one smile from this lovely woman. Part of me wanted to flee, part of me wanted to rake her beautiful eyes out.

Light as a feather, but solid as stone, I thought of option C.

"Yes, and you are Eve's Apple Red."

A flash of confusion furrowed her brow, but then the full lips bloomed into a smile of true delight. "Oh my! I am indeed. I

guess you must be used to Sander's fans. I'm one of his biggest—
he does wonderful work." Marsha's voice slid over me like warm
molasses, slow, sweet, sultry and thick.

Maybe I shouldn't have been surprised by the various
tentacles of jealousy, but this feeling was new. I was jealous of
Sander, that he had found this beautiful sensual woman, had
known her before I met her. I stepped into Marsha's warmth,
the sleeve of her silk blouse cool against my forearm. I looked
into hazel-green eyes, the irises like anchors inside delicate
golden sunbursts. I didn't see myself reflected within them,
but I wanted to. I reached up to her face, an intimate and bold
gesture, but Marsha didn't flinch, the flames in her eyes blaring
bright with curiosity. With my fingertips a cloud on her cheek,
my thumb touched the red velvet softness of her lower lip, her
expression cool, calm.

"We would be delighted if you came to dinner tonight, six
p.m."

Her gaze stayed steady on mine, and the full lower lip thinned
slightly as her lips turned gently up. "I'll bring dessert."

Voices drifted into the studio and broke the spell, one being
Sander's. My hand fell away from Marsha's face and I walked
on air toward my husband, my pussy wet, my heart racing. He
didn't look guilty, but pleasantly surprised to see me. "Come by
for lunch?"

I smiled and kissed him lightly, my Seashell Pink not leaving
a trace. "That was my intent, but," I looked over my shoulder
to Marsha, her head nodding sagely as she spoke to the director,
"our plans have changed. Dinner's at six. Do not be late."

Before he could say a word, I kissed him again, sliding my
tongue into his mouth, a tease, a wicked, arousing promise he'd
have to deal with all afternoon. I stepped outside his arms as
they reached to encircle me, my pussy tingling with arousal,

with want and with that glorious almost forgotten fire that was anticipation.

I had a lot of work to do before dinner, and I was beyond starving.

We moved into the living room, Marsha and I settling on the couch. Sander joined us with three brandies cradled in his hands. He sat in the leather-upholstered chair by Marsha.

Dinner had passed in a haze of sweet tension, with Sander charming and unable to completely conceal an almost youthful discomfort. A sliver of playful pity tickled me as Marsha and I enjoyed the fruits of our sexual sorority, subtle innuendo peppering the dinner conversation, and there, Sander, looking between us, unsure of the shifting ground. Marsha hadn't disappointed me in her attire, a sheer black silk blouse, the bustier underneath an embroidered masterpiece. Black sheer stockings painted her long legs, her heels red as her signature lips—the same sinful shade I also wore. The current of desire seared the air between the three of us, and while Marsha and I never spoke of arrangements or expectations, I knew there was no doubt the evening would end however I wanted it to.

I held the brandy in my hand a moment before I set it aside, unwilling to dull the moment, riding high on the slick pulse of my clit and the thrum in my veins. One look at Sander and I knew we shared the same invigoration. Any apprehensions I had wrestled with while making dinner vanished with that look at my husband, to see that spark that had been banked in both of us. And Marsha, sitting with her legs elegantly crossed at her ankles, the snifter held in nails painted the same Eve's Apple Red.

I didn't know how far things might go, but I wasn't ruling anything out. I reveled in the unknown and took the reins. I stood

up and retrieved the remote for the music system. With a deft
thumb, a tenor sax began to sway soulfully. Instead of returning
to my seat, I went to Sander, leaned over him and kissed him
with that same promising slip of tongue, then I pulled away to
stand in front of Marsha, her black hair shining in the glow
of candles I'd scattered throughout the living room and dining
room. Marsha smiled at me, the flames of her irises molten and
open. I melted to the floor, kneeling before her, my hands in my
lap as we just stared at each other for a long moment. When my
fingers finally touched her, I shivered, wanting, basking in the
frozen, lustful gaze of my husband, tangible as a stroke though
he watched from the periphery.

Marsha's heat branded me. My fingers didn't tremble, I was
proud of that, as I traced lines up her legs. My breath hitched at
the sensation of the silky stockings on the pads of my fingers. I'd
worn silk stockings, I'd smoothed them over my own legs often,
but this was so different, so erotically foreign that my head
swam for a moment. My hands moved on, over her skirt, the
material a barrier I needed to melt away. At her waist, the sheer
blouse whispered against my hands as I traced the embroidery
pattern of the bustier, and my nimble fingers unfastened the
buttons. She leaned forward to help me remove the shirt, and I
saw creamy skin lightly dusted with freckles on her shoulders.
When Marsha tipped my chin up with her fingertips, a wave of
fear washed over me, but as she kissed me, everything around
me, in me, turned golden. Her mouth was generous, her tongue
a mentor as she lead me through the whole ecstatic moment.
The fall was thrilling, stole my breath and melted me from the
inside out. My pussy clenched against the crash of pleasure,
edging me toward orgasm.

With my loving Sander watching.

When Marsha stood to step out of her skirt, she rose and

radiated vitality, wisdom, sexuality eternal. I sat on my heels and looked at her, fearful she'd vanish and the moment would blow away like river mist in the face of a rising sun. When I kissed her thigh, the lacy edge of her garter brushed against my cheek, an odd affirmation of reality. She sighed as my lips trailed kisses to her hip, my hands sliding up the backs of her legs to cup her firm ass.

She reached down and lifted me up and in a short order, my clothes were scattered with hers. I stood in my bra and thong feeling sexier, more alive than I had in ages, and when Sander stood and ran his hands over my arms, I nearly came. It was a seamless meld, no awkwardness or missteps as Sander became our center, Marsha and I at his sides, but partially facing each other.

Sander, silent, his eyes a rage of want, traced his thumb along my spine, and I knew he touched Marsha in some similar fashion. He didn't ask my permission, but I saw reassurance smooth the crease between his eyes. His cock pitched forward, a comical tent of arousal and a dark spot betraying the silky pearl he'd already released.

Marsha and I worked together to remove Sander's clothing, our lips tasting his skin, our hands caressing him, caressing each other, as we cast our spell, transforming him into a legendary lover, Tristan with two Isoldes. Traces of Eve marked his chest, his thighs, the top of his left foot (that was me...Sander has such sensitive feet), and with the slightest nod to Marsha, I slid behind him, out of his embrace, and encircled his chest with my arms. Marsha kissed his lips once, a tender exchange, then squatted before him, her fingers circling his erect prick, then stroked slowly, as she guided his cock to the bow of her mouth, the Eve's Apple Red a glorious ring around his hard, veined flesh. She licked and traced his length with her tongue tip, and torturously slid his cock in and out of her mouth.

I watched from behind him, my hands caressing his chest, thrilled at the rocketing heartbeat beneath my hands, my teeth nipping his shoulders and his back as Marsha tested his restraint with her beautiful mouth. And there, Eve tattooed his cock.

She pulled away before he could come, met my gaze and grinned, wiping a drop of saliva from her lower lip. Stretching like a cat, she took a pillow from the couch and soon she lay on the carpet, stroking down her body. I slid away from Sander and settled on the carpet between Marsha's legs. I leaned to kiss her, nothing tentative, a passionate, bruising bite that she met with equal verve. Her nipples teased the edges of the bustier, her stretched body releasing her sweet breasts from their cups. I kissed each nipple, my teeth raking the sensitive flesh, and before I could release the second, warm hands caressed my back, Sander behind me, his tortured cock a welcome rod against my ass.

I moved down Marsha's body, my fingers exploring her skin at the edges of the bustier, working with the snaps of her garters as she arched to meet my kisses, my touch. As her fingers tangled in my hair, my fingers slid beneath the black satin of her panties, reveling in the wet heat of her pussy. And behind me, Sander's fingers slid into the folds of mine, my juices slicking his course. We were one, such an incredible sense of unity, of bond, three people, one divine, orgiastic goal.

I slid Marsha's panties over her hips and Sander followed my lead, removing my thong with a savage snap of elastic. His fingers plunged into my pussy, and I rocketed toward orgasm. With Marsha's panties off, I admired the neatly trimmed bush and circled her stiff clit with my fingers and teasingly slid two in, pumping, each plunge deeper. Marsha's breathing became more labored, and I wanted to taste her orgasm, I wanted that intimacy that only my lips could offer. She'd stained my husband's cock with her apple red shade, it was only right I stain her cunt the same way.

At first, my tongue was tentative, a flick of the tip like I might test the frosting on a gourmet cupcake. I savored the delicate spice of her juices, the warm, exotic scent that enveloped me as I explored every fold. I lapped her clit until her body was trembling and she panted with escalating pleasure.

I dripped. Sander's fingers knew me so well, and now, excited beyond reason, he exploited me, teasing my pussy until I groaned into Marsha's. He slipped his fingers deep into me, then removed them so I almost crumbled with the vacancy. When he finally put his cock in me, I came, hard, fast, full and blinding, crying out, trembling with the overwhelming shock of it, but before I could collapse into the moment, he gripped my hair, tugged me back, and I continued my assault on Marsha's pussy, my mouth watering, my tongue less coordinated, but no less direct.

And Sander fucked me—fucked me hard, slamming into my body, filling me with his cock, his heart, every fiber of his sexual being and I bloomed under the assault. My mouth flooded with Marsha's orgasm, her cry of bliss a song of such completion tears burned my eyes. As Sander's cock pistoned in and out and his fingers relentlessly rubbed and tweaked my clit, another climax rose in me, a massive wave I wondered if I would survive. Just a beat, a single pulse of tiny wings, and I shattered into a powder of sensation so fine, so pure it spread across a mile of nerves and breath. It mixed with Marsha's and with Sander's hot releases as our trio of voices drowned the music, drowned everything but the magic of three bodies and one shared ecstasy.

We spooned, Sander sandwiched between Marsha and me. No words had been spoken since the brandy. None were needed.

We all wore the same badge, the same smeared lip color, red dashes on skin and of course, one crimson-ringed cock.

Our color, tonight and on nights to come, the sign and signal of our shared intentions—Eve's Apple Red.

EXPERIENCE
AND
EXPECTATIONS

Kathleen Tudor

I just don't see the point," Jennifer says, reciting her usual line in our broken record of a conversation.

"It's softer than a toy, but harder, too. More pliable, but firmer," I say by rote, not even listening to her standard reply, *That makes no sense.* As soon as the sound of her voice fades away, I give her my answer, as soft and well-worn as an old pair of boots. "It's just something you have to experience to understand."

I pick at my salad—why, oh why did I order a salad?—while I wait for Jennifer to ask me why she would need to experience a man when a woman gives her everything she could ever want. My lunch is like torture, and I'm starving as I pick through the lettuce for *real* food. Cheese. Croutons. Tiny fragments of bacon. I was trying to forestall the *You should eat healthier* discussion, and got *Why does any woman need a man?,* instead.

But Jennifer hesitates, breaking the skipping-record rhythm of our familiar conversation. Finally, as hesitantly as a virgin, she asks, "Doesn't it hurt? I've heard—"

I carefully set down my fork, focusing on laying it perfectly straight to keep from laughing. "In this case," I finally say, "there's not much a man could do to you that I haven't performed some variation of, already. Think of it as a new toy, but with a guy attached."

She blushes even though I've managed to keep a straight face. "I've just—you always seem so—you have this smug air of satisfaction when you talk about...it. Do you really think—do you *really* think I'd enjoy it, too?" She won't lift her eyes from her soup, which is probably good, because I'd guess that my eyes are bugging out. Jennifer has been a proud lesbian since she started growing body hair, and had even been known to flaunt her gold star in certain situations, though she has never treated me as "lesser" because I'm bi.

I swallow the million things I could be saying, and take a sip of sparkling water to give myself a moment. "Well," I say at last, "I usually have. Jen, where's this coming from?"

"I don't know, I've just been thinking about it a lot lately. About things you've described while you're teasing me. For the first time, I guess I actually started to wonder if I'm missing anything." She meets my eyes at last. "And you think you could set something up? Just for the one time, mind you? Just to see?"

I nod, showing her with my expression that I understand the gravity of her request. "I know someone."

"Okay." She picks up her spoon and takes a sip of her soup. Have I noticed the ridiculously cheap lawn furniture the neighbors put in their backyard, this year? The topic is dropped, but my mind continues to spin.

Nick is a member of the kayaking meet-up I attend once a month, but we formed a bit of a bond early on, and regularly call each other for less crowded days out on the bay. "Hey, Maddy," he says when I call him, and I can hear the smile in his voice and a sound like wind in the background. "I was just thinking of you. The weather's supposed to be fine this weekend; *tell* me you're up for a little recreation."

"I am," I say, smiling back, "but not the kind you're thinking of."

He pauses, and I can almost hear the gears turning. "Hike?" He sounds mystified.

"Do you remember that picture I showed you of my wife?"

"Jennifer, right? You're one lucky bitch. Why?"

"Yeah," I agree to both his statements at once. "We've been talking, and she wants to try some...*recreation*...with a guy."

There is a long silence as he determines that I don't mean camping. Then a squeak, "What, *me*?"

"You're hot, you're single and you're attracted to both of us. Sounds like a recipe for some fun," I say casually. I don't add that I already know he's generously appointed. He never realized that I witnessed the entirety of his wetsuit debacle last summer, and I don't plan to embarrass him.

"I feel like there must be some sort of catch. Or maybe I'm misunderstanding something..."

"Nick," I say sweetly, "Would you please come over this Saturday and fuck my wife and me silly? She'd like to give stallions a fair shot, at least once."

Even over the noise of wind in the background, I can hear Nick swallow. "What time should I be there?"

Jennifer goes crazy trying to prepare for Nick's arrival. She spends two days cleaning everything in sight, and I stay out of her way, since every attempt to help seems to get me snapped at. She vacillates between manic excitement and complete panic, and eventually, I just give up trying to calm her down.

Saturday morning, she can't decide whether she should get dressed or just put on a sexy nightie. What does one wear for a prearranged booty call? Instead of offering suggestions, I put on a summery yellow sundress and make sure Jennifer sees me. She sags in relief and dives into the closet to find one of her own girly numbers: a strapless denim dress that fits like it was made for her.

"Maddy?" she calls from the closet, "Are you wearing panties? Should I be wearing panties?" She pokes her head out, still adjusting the dress. "If I don't wear panties, will he think I'm slutty?" I kiss her and assure her that sluttiness is the whole point, for today.

I've only just gotten her settled at the kitchen table with a cup of tea when the doorbell rings, and Jennifer jumps up, nearly spilling it. She rushes for the door, stops after three steps, glances back at me, and then turns back to the door, frozen. "I can't do this," she whispers.

"You're going to love it," I whisper back. I kiss her stiff lips, and she softens after a moment, warming beneath my touch as she always does. I want to kiss her boneless, but Nick is waiting. I go to let him in.

"Maddy!" He kisses my cheek before he passes the threshold, and then he turns his eyes to Jennifer and smiles sweetly at her. His checks are stained slightly pink as he says, "You both look beautiful."

"Would you like something to eat? Drink?" she asks, breathless. She's panicking again.

I give Nick what I hope is an encouraging smile, and move to stand in front of Jennifer. I take her face in my hands, forcing her to look deep into my eyes. After a moment, she's breathing along with me, slow and deep.

This time, I do kiss her until she's boneless. Her lips open sweetly under my steady assault, and I sweep my tongue across them, making her shiver and go almost limp in my arms. Then I gesture Nick over and slip sideways out of her grasp. He takes over smoothly, as if we had planned it, and though Jennifer jumps when his lips meet hers, he soon has her moaning into his kisses. I *knew* he would be good.

I watch for as long as I can stand it, but soon my hands are itching for more. My nipples stand out against the cotton of my dress, pebbled and aching, and my face feels as flushed as the juncture of my legs. I move behind Nick and reach around him to unbutton his sport shirt, letting my fingers graze his lightly furred chest and belly.

It's Jennifer who reaches to push the shirt off of his shoulders, running her palms over the contours of his chest and abs as she explores the alien frontier. I toss the shirt away and join her, enjoying the smooth, clean lines of his body and the little beads of his nipples. It's his turn to moan as our hands roam across his hard body, our fingers occasionally meeting, tangling, parting.

I press myself against his back, inhaling the familiar scent of him in a context so unexpected that I am afraid sunshine and wetsuits will flip my switches from now on. The skin of his shoulder is warm and soft beneath my lips—firm. I nip at the flesh there and feel him shiver. I like it. I run my tongue from the top of his shoulder up the side of his neck, and he breaks the kiss to gasp, his head falling back.

Jennifer stands, panting, and gives him the up and down. "Do men like…?" She reaches for him and pinches one of his nipples between slender fingers. He lets out a groan so deep it is almost a growl, and captures her hand, pulling it gently toward the front of his Bermuda shorts.

"Does it feel like I like…?"

"Oh," she breathes. "Yes…" I let my nails graze over Nick's back as he stands, patient and trembling, letting Jennifer explore the unfamiliar hardness at her own pace. His hands clench at his sides, and he sucks in a breath. Jennifer smiles shyly. "Could I…see?"

"God, yes!" His shorts vanish so fast, I almost think they could be tear-away. Nick hasn't bothered with underpants, either. The observation makes me smile, and the frankly curious expression on Jennifer's face makes it broaden.

"Gorgeous," I say quietly. He's even more impressive than I'd assumed from my sneak preview of his flaccid state, which is saying something, since he impressed me even then. I step around him to run a fingertip up and down his length, and he takes a slow, deep breath.

It's too tempting. Jennifer and I have been together for four years, and I haven't tasted a cock since a few months before *that*. I settle onto my knees in front of him as Jennifer cedes her place to me, and Nick's groan is almost wild as I suck his tip gently into my mouth, caressing the softness of his head with my swirling tongue. His hand brushes through my hair, gently cupping the back of my head, and he caresses me without forcing. How refreshingly polite!

I reward him by taking him deeper, bobbing my head slowly up and down his thick shaft. We have a toy as broad as him— we call it the monster.

I can hear both of them breathing, both fast and deep, Nick gasping occasionally when I hit a particularly sensitive spot, Jennifer nearly panting with desire. For me? For him? For all of it?

She kneels behind me and brushes my hair over my shoulder so she can reach the straps of my dress, which tie halter-style behind my neck. She pulls the ties ever so slowly, letting my own motion do some of the work for her until they fall free at last. My dress drops down to my waist, baring my breasts, and she presses up against me from behind, lifting them. Teasing them. She tweaks my nipple and I moan deep in my throat, making sure Nick gets a jolt from the vibration. His groan joins the chorus of pleasure.

Jennifer teases and tweaks and massages until I'm whimpering, which admittedly doesn't take long, then she pushes my dress down past my hips and traces one hand back up my thigh toward my pussy. I swallow hard around Nick's cock. He swears softly, and his hand on the back of my head gives a twitch. It makes me laugh, at least until the gentle stroke between my lips and across my clit chokes me off with a gasp.

Behind me, I can feel Jennifer pushing her own dress up to her waist, and she presses the back of her wrist into my ass to demonstrate that she's stroking herself exactly the same as she's stroking me. I suck harder, losing myself in the familiar dance of pleasure as she slowly brings both of us toward our peaks, and gasp in surprise as Nick steps back, pulling his cock out of my reach.

"I don't want to—" he gestures to himself. "Anyway, I'd like to watch, if I can?"

I wait for Jennifer to demur, but she says nothing, only goes on kissing my neck and stroking both our pussies in time. "Yes," I gasp, speaking to both of them. I tug my dress away from my knees so that I can spread my legs, giving him a better view—and her better access.

Jennifer dips a finger between my lips and sends it inside my hot core, and I moan as she presses the pad of her hand against my clit. Aroused and left with nothing else to occupy me, I cup my breasts, massaging them gently and catching my nipples between my fingers, twisting just enough.

Nick watches, his cock bobbing softly with his pulse, his eyes wide, as my wife pleasures us both. Her breath hitches behind my ear and she begins to tremble, losing her steady rhythm, but the knowledge of her ecstasy is enough to push me across that last gap and tip me into the heavens, and we fill the air with soft, feminine cries and sweet sighs of content.

"Jesus," Nick breathes.

I have to swallow twice before my mouth feels dry enough to speak. "I think we should take this to the bedroom now." I stand and offer Jennifer my hand.

In the bedroom, I unzip the denim dress and let it fall away, stripping my gorgeous wife of her final barrier. I lead her to the bed and lie down beside her, kissing her deeply as Nick lies down on her other side to fondle her breasts, and then to suckle at them, one and then the other.

"Do you like that?" I whisper.

"It's...different. I can feel his beard—Oh!" He's discovered that she likes to be bit. I grin at him, and he grins back wickedly before he does it again, eliciting more cries of pleasure. Then he reaches between Jennifer's legs. She tenses, capturing his hand with her thighs, and he freezes, looking at me.

"Do you want to stop?" I ask gently. Poor Nick, I know he'll stop if she asks him to, but his balls will be cerulean. I wonder, briefly, if she'll let me fuck him if she won't do it.

But she takes a deep breath and relaxes. "I'm sorry. I've just never had a man touch me there before..."

Nick places a kiss on her pubic bone, just above the short, sandy-brown curls, and I feel a shudder go all the way through her. I place one hand gently on her face, focusing her on me, and kiss her deeply, letting my tongue wander and plunder at will. She moans, and I feel the last of the tension release.

Nick shifts. Jennifer's leg tangles with mine as she opens. I trace swirls across her chest, and Jennifer takes a deep breath through her nose, letting it out in a soft whimper into my mouth as her hips thrust upward.

"That's right," Nick murmurs, and I wonder if it's a mistake, reminding her that he's there, and that he's oh-so-male, but Jennifer moans and her hips buck again as he continues. "God, you're so wet. So hot and tight. Damn, you're sexy. I love it when you moan like that. You want it all, don't you?"

Jennifer gasps against my lips and I pull away, watching her face as her mouth falls open and her eyes roll back. I lay my palm flat on the center of her chest and feel the tremors within her as she arches off the bed and freezes. Between her legs, Nick has two fingers inside her, and is fucking her with a gentle, insistent rhythm, the rough pad of his thumb scraping along her clit in time. But even as he concentrates on keeping pace, his other hand is trying to tear a condom free from the strip I'd laid on the bedside table. I take it, tear the package open and pass it back.

He meets my eyes and smiles, and as he rolls it smoothly down over his erection, we both turn to watch Jennifer shatter. She jerks twice, like she's been electrocuted, and a moan tears from her throat, long and drawn out.

Nick is over her in an instant, covering his body with hers as he braces his athletic body on one arm. The other arm is lowered, grasping his cock firmly, positioning it at her entrance. He waits with steady calm, but I can see the sweat beading on his forehead. I want to lean forward and lick it off, so I do. He smiles, but doesn't take his eyes off of Jennifer's face.

She trembles again, still whimpering and moaning, and her eyes flutter open. "What are you waiting for?"

"You," he says, and I want to laugh at the roughness of his voice. He must be on the very edge of control.

She doesn't look like she understands, so I step in to save him. "Do you want him to fuck you, baby?"

Jennifer looks at me. "Yes." Then back at him. "Yes! Fuck me—" She breaks off on a cry as he thrusts once, twice, thrice, until he is seated completely within her. Her eyes are wide and I nearly purr as I imagine what she must be feeling as she experiences the velvety smooth, pliant hardness of a man's cock for the first time—and a stallion of a man, at that. She must be feeling that subtle stretch, as if he's about to tear her apart, but not as harsh as a plastic toy, or a glass one. Not as sharp.

Nick shifts, bringing one knee up, pushing at her legs, and Jennifer complies, letting him wrap her legs over his shoulders until he can drive into her. I've already warned him not to bother with slow and sweet with my spicy Jen, and he's taken it to heart. He gives her a moment to adjust, followed by a few smooth, teasing thrusts that touch on the edges of pleasure, but do nothing to drive her toward it...

Then he begins to fuck her in earnest. Nick holds himself above my wife and pounds into her, eliciting an endless stream of moans and whimpers and yelps. He turns toward me, and I know what he wants. I lift myself up to him and press my lips against his, holding his head steady as our kiss turns passionate and sharp. I reach between their bodies and form a ring of my finger and thumb, milking Nick every time he thrusts through it. And each time he slams down, he forces the base of my thumb into Jennifer's clit.

The tenor of her cries changes as my hand massages her toward orgasm. Nick and I are both breathing hard, panting into the kiss that we refuse to break, though I sense that he can't last much longer. And then he doesn't have to. Jennifer, still sensitive, gives a strangled gasp and convulses beneath us, totally lost in the shock of the pleasure. Nick breaks the kiss to let out a ragged growl, and his cock pulses and surges in my hand as he thrusts a couple more times, then pulls away.

I kiss Jennifer until her eyes uncross and her breathing returns to normal, and we both look up to see Nick standing at the side of the bed looking strangely shy. "Well?" he asks.

Jennifer laughs. "Not bad, thank you. Would you like to stay for lunch?"

I pinch her side playfully. "None of that! *One* of you is absolutely going to have to play with me until he's ready to give me *my* turn."

They both grin and turn on me, and as four hands begin to tease every part of my body, I realize that my turn will not be a problem.

THE MISTRESS IN THE BRAT

Skylar Kade

Don't be a brat, Ginny. You know that doesn't fly with me."

I had been hearing that all too often lately. As usual, it cut to my heart but damn if I could stop myself from acting out. Omar and I had, for five years now, the kind of blissfully perfect relationship that had all our friends rolling their eyes.

That had been in the years Before the Changes. Before I'd been given that corner window office I'd sought during my tenure at my network infrastructure company in Silicon Valley. Before our lover found her own Dom and left us. Before our newest play partner, Sasha, moved back home to care for her ailing mother.

Now, all we did was butt heads. Not because of my long hours, because that hadn't been anything new, but because I couldn't seem to transition from ball-busting VP to the sweet submissive he was used to. Our life was as ill fitting as a washed wool sweater.

Silent, I let my eyes plead with Omar. I needed his love and understanding. Something. I was groping in the dark, alone in a way I hadn't been in the years since I'd met my lover and partner and Dom. Just when he was supposed to be by my side to flick on that light switch, he was, instead, my adversary. He shook his head and sighed at me before leaving the room. I knew better than to follow—he needed space to gather his thoughts.

It was Friday night, our standing date for the weekly BDSM house party we attended outside the city proper. He'd set out a violently violet corset I normally loved to wear, but when I had come home—late, again—to see his choice of outfit on the bed, I had ignored it. Normally, I couldn't care less what I wore, but at that moment, the corset had been more than distasteful. It rankled that he'd chosen my outfit, though it never had before.

So I pulled on a strappy black top instead. Miscalculation on my part. Not because of the punishment I knew awaited me, but because of the disappointment that had crinkled the corner of his full lips.

Footsteps heavy in his steel-toed boots, Omar returned and towered over me. He'd always been taller than me, but I hadn't felt small, deep in my soul, until that moment.

The gut reaction to sink to my knees and bow my head warred with the irrational defiance that had grown in me these past months. Fuck if I could figure out a way to excise it, because if I could, I would in a heartbeat. I would do anything for this man.

Except wear a corset of his choosing. It seemed a small concession right now, yet I wouldn't back down.

"Do you even want to go tonight?" His dark eyes shuttered like a beach house closing up for winter, leaving me cold and empty.

I swallowed the bile that rose as I dropped into my rest position, knees spread and palms up on my thighs. I railed at the deference even as I spoke. "Yes, Sir."

His sigh was heavy enough that it weighed me down. "Ten spanks as punishment for the corset. As for the rest," his shoulders slumped as he took a seat on our overstuffed brown suede couch, "I'm still working on that."

I lay over his thighs and counted out my punishment, but the pain didn't take the edge off the itch under my skin.

Something had to give, and soon. I just hoped it wasn't our relationship.

After an awkwardly silent ride to the club, I managed to take my place a half step behind Sir as we entered the house. My eyes stayed glued to the ground until he found us a seat on one of the low-slung couches scattered through the main floor. Once I was settled on my knees by his feet, I let my attention wander around the room.

The usual crowd was in attendance; most of the regulars were our friends. Their scenes, under normal circumstances, turned me on, thrilled every chamber of my submissive little heart.

Not tonight. To be honest, it had been a while since the ambiance had really affected me.

My head slumped forward in defeat. What was wrong with me?

From the corner of my eye, I spied a familiar pair of spike heels. Sasha. Blood thrummed through my veins.

She sank to her knees with a blonde, angelic grace that turned me on, just like it had the first time we'd played with her. Omar had loved topping both of us. The sex, once he and I had returned home, was fantastic.

"Hello, honey. It's good to see you again." Omar's voice poured over me like warm, sticky syrup. That heat had been missing from all our recent conversations and jealousy clawed at my chest.

"Sir. It's good to be home." Sasha looked up at him and smiled.

Before I could think, my hand shot out and grabbed a fistful of her hair. "No eye contact without permission, girl." I yanked until she was looking at his boots. Just because I had trouble following protocol didn't mean she got to play fast and loose with the rules—and my man.

"Yes, Mistress." The words flew from Sasha's mouth.

Mistress? Satisfaction curled through me. Her instant submission was a heady power trip and when I locked eyes with Omar, he wore a dangerously speculative expression.

With one long finger, he hooked my collar and yanked me close to him. "You like that, don't you?"

I nodded and averted my eyes, letting myself sink into the control that rolled off him. It was like coming home. "Yes, Sir."

A tug later, and I was on my feet next to Sasha. Omar leaned over my shoulder and whispered in my ear. "Tell her to crawl behind you."

I did. She obeyed. Desire flared low in my stomach.

Like a row of ducklings, we followed Omar to an unoccupied room in the house. This whole floor was filled with kink furniture, tie-downs and more surfaces to fuck on than the average deviant mind could conjure up.

It was the best weekend escape anyone could hope for, and the longer I was here tonight, the better I felt. It was like taking off a tight bra after a long day. I could breathe again.

Omar grabbed me by the hair and forced me into the huge wooden chair that took center stage in this room. "Over her knee, Sasha."

Oh my god. Sasha's long, tanned limbs sprawled across me. She wore a crop top, sans bra, and an obscenely short skirt over neon-pink panties. The skirt flared up to expose the full curves of her ass, the muscled flesh of her thighs. I stroked a hand up and down, knee to lower back. She twitched on my lap.

"What's our safeword, honey?"

"Red, Sir." Her voice was already tinged with a dream-like quality.

The few times we'd played with her, she'd hurtled into subspace. Evidently, that was a rarity for her—though I understood. Omar had that effect on me, too.

"Sasha, we're going to welcome you home properly. Ginny, I think twenty spanks should do it." Omar moved behind the chair and loomed over my shoulder. I bet he loved this view.

Sasha and I had been tied up together, had kissed, had cuddled after a long scene. I had never topped her, though. I'd never had my fingers or tongue buried in her cunt, either, but that now held infinite appeal. I could control her pleasure and damn if that didn't make me hot.

For now, though, I obeyed Omar.

After the first five slaps, I rubbed her pink cheeks, then nudged her knees apart. My fingers dipped between her legs— she was soaked. We both gasped. I explored, tracing the lines of her pussy lips through her panties until I met her clit. She bucked in my lap.

A firm hand on my neck made me freeze. "Bad girl." Omar's teasing admonishment slithered over my skin. "I told you to spank her."

Though I didn't want to stop, I would—for him. The remaining fifteen spanks I peppered over her ass and thighs, until Sasha was grinding on my lap and begging me to touch her again.

If we continued, I knew we'd be broaching new territory. When we started scening with Sasha, she had been looking for mentorship. For experience submitting.

This would be something else entirely.

Dizzy with the possibilities unfolding, I looked up to Omar. "Sir?"

He knew me well enough—I didn't need to say anything else. He nodded.

"Sasha? Do you want more?" I let my fingers tease over the gusset of her underwear and waited for her reply.

"Yes, please, Ma'am!"

My fingers tugged at her panties and she helped, kind of, squirming in my lap until the offending piece of clothing dropped to the floor. I could see the plump lips of her labia, shining with her arousal.

Without preamble, my fingers delved into her, first one, then another, until she devolved to incoherent babbling.

Had begging ever sounded so sweet? Was this the rush Omar felt when I submitted?

Omar dropped to his knees at Sasha's head and muffled her with deep kisses. Damn, that was hot. He pulled her hair and her cries jumped an octave. Her pussy clamped down around my fingers, squeezing so tight I could barely move them, and her body shook on my lap.

When she'd relaxed, I withdrew from her body and Sir picked her up in his arms, then sank onto the comfortable settee in the opposite corner of the room. Together, we soothed her, brought her down. She was sprawled across Omar's lap, but her head rested in mine. I stroked her hair as he rubbed a big hand up and down her legs.

"Ginny, get her a bottle of water."

I didn't balk at the command. Instead, I resettled Sasha so

she rested against the crook of his arm and rose.

"Crawl for me, baby." His order, whip sharp, hit that primal part of me that had been lately obscured. I dropped to the floor and obeyed. With every movement, my clit rubbed against my panties.

Coolers with water bottles sat outside each playroom, so I didn't have far to go. As I traversed the distance, I could feel myself falling into the familiar rhythm of submission. This time, I didn't put up a fight.

Water bottle held in my teeth, I returned to Sir's side. Using my best form, I presented the water bottle to him.

Satisfaction shone in his eyes. He patted the couch and I returned to my earlier position. I traced Sasha's thick lower lip. Her tongue flickered out lazily, to swipe across the pad of my thumb. Sir inhaled sharply, and said, "I don't think we're close to done for the evening. Is that okay, honey?"

Sasha, through fluttering eyelids, looked up at him, then locked eyes with me. "I am more than okay with that. I think it might be up to Ginny. Ma'am?"

That didn't require a second's extra thought to decide. "Absolutely."

Sir leaned over and dropped a kiss on my forehead. "Don't think you're getting out of your own punishment, baby."

I scowled.

"Save it for your subbie-girl," he replied.

Mine. Possession roared through me—for him, for her.

After Sasha returned to her normal cognizant state, we agreed to return to our home. Sir situated me in the backseat with Sasha and before closing the door, he instructed me to play with her the whole ride home.

Now, as we pulled into the garage, I was power-drunk and

Sasha was squirming against the confines of her seat belt and the wrist cuffs I'd buckled her into. That had been a heady rush, hearing the click of the buckles, watching her adjust to the weight of the leather cuffs, and knowing I'd done that to her.

"Out of the car, girls." Sir's deep voice was as seductive as a hand pulling my hair. I scrambled through the car door and into the house. From behind, I heard the smack of flesh on flesh and Sasha's yelp. Slowpoke.

A grin took my mouth, wider and truer than any I'd felt in weeks. She had a lot to learn—I just hoped she wanted to stick around long enough to do so.

He instructed us to head to the playroom and strip. I showed Sasha down to the basement, and into the locked half of the floor that held all our toys and furniture.

We hadn't been down here in weeks. Guilt sucked at my joy, but I clamped it down. This could be a new beginning. A fresh start.

Sasha revealed her glorious, curvy body and my heart swelled. I'd missed her while she was gone. Though we'd only played a few times, we had chemistry. Sasha and me, the two of us submitting to Omar as equals. And when she'd had to go home, I thought that was the last we'd see of her.

She was back. With us. In our playroom.

Mine.

I shed my clothes and pressed myself to her bare back. She hissed in a breath. My hands explored the canvas of her body, noting how sensitive she was at the crook of her arm, the way she cried out and canted her hips back when I scored my nails across her stomach. With a hand tangled in her short brown hair, I tugged and exposed the long line of her neck. When she whimpered, I set my teeth into the juncture of her neck and shoulder. She bucked in my arms and I held her still with my arm across her hip, my fingers dipping into the wetness between her legs.

"Getting started without me?"

I looked up to see Sir in his favorite black jeans, slung low on his hips. His coffee-colored skin shone in the diffuse overhead light and he looked so edible I wanted to drop to my knees, release the erection that was pressing against the zipper of his pants and beg him to fuck my mouth.

Sasha's lusty perusal indicated she would love to join me.

He growled. "Not yet, girls."

Sasha sagged, leaning back against my chest and sinking deeper onto my fingers. She shuddered, and I reveled in her reaction.

"Here's how we're going to play this." He stalked across the space and stroked his hand up my arm, leaving goose bumps in its wake. "I'm going to get you two set up, then let you play. I'll step in and do what I like, when I like. Aside from that," he said, nipping my earlobe, "you're in control, Ginny."

Chills zipped up my spine.

He moved and grabbed Sasha by the throat. Her eyes fluttered closed in bliss. This was, as she'd told us the first time we played, one of her submissive triggers. "Are you going to be a good girl for Mistress Ginny?"

My pussy clenched at the title, then again when Sasha said, "Yes, Sir."

"Put her on the spanking horse, baby." He let her go, then propped himself up on the wall.

With more skin contact than was necessary, I laid Sasha's supple body over the padded, waist-high horse. Where Sir was hard and muscled, Sasha had soft, smooth skin—breasts that overflowed my palms, an ass that begged for a handprint and hips that enticed me to drag my nails down her sides. She was a sensual feast, and she was mine for the night. Longer, if I was lucky.

"You might want to cuff her down," Sir suggested.

Each clink of metal clipping into place drew a whimper from Sasha. Once she was secured in her bent-over position, Sir pushed away from the wall and selected one of the crops that hung nearby. This one had a stiff round leather top with a heart cutout.

"Use this." He handed off the toy and retreated.

I warmed up her skin with my hands, rubbing circles over her ass and thighs until her tanned skin took on a rosy hue. Then I brought the crop down on the fleshy curve of her butt. She jumped but stayed silent.

"Hit her harder—you know she craves it. If you don't, you'll find yourself on the receiving end of that crop."

The second swing cracked through the room. Sasha's yelp faded into a moan, and our pattern was established: swing-smack-cry-gasp over and over until I lost track of time and Sasha's backside was covered in red hearts.

"Enough." The word barely penetrated the haze of my joy, but once it did I stepped back and into Sir's hard chest. "Good girl. Look at what you've done to her, how eager she is for your touch. How obedient she's been."

Her fingers curled around the legs of the horse in a death grip and her body vibrated with pent-up tension.

"You still need your punishment, baby. Are you ready?"

I stuttered. "We're just going to leave her there? Needing?"

He gave me an assessing look. "That's up to you. Do you want to make her wait for her pleasure, or give it to her now?"

I thought about what he would do in the situation, what brought me the most pleasure when I was under his control. A wicked thought wiggled through my mind. "I have an idea, Sir."

With a wave of his hand, he gestured for me to grab whatever I needed. I hurried around the room and grabbed the items, then returned. With a hand on Sasha's lower back to steady her, I set the vibrator at her entrance and fucked it into her body. She sobbed and tried to take it in deeper but I made her wait. Once it was inside, I turned up the power and the head of the rabbit vibe started to rotate as the external tips hummed along her clit.

"You're not allowed to come, honey," I rasped in her ear.

At that, she squirmed against her bonds. "No, Mistress, please!"

I snagged her panties from the floor next to her feet, where I'd dropped them, and maneuvered her until I could slide them back up her legs to hold the toy in place.

Then, with Sir's hand in my hair, I let myself be dragged into her line of sight. "Not only are you not allowed to come," he rumbled, "but you have to watch Ginny's punishment. Don't close your eyes, or look away, or you're next."

She shuddered, and I let his voice wash over me as I sank into the shallow end of the subspace pool. Sir buckled me to the Saint Andrew's cross in the corner, directly in Sasha's line of sight. I tugged at the cuffs—good and trapped. Hot.

I waited until he returned with whatever implement he chose for my punishment. Sasha gasped and worry trickled through my mind.

"Are you going to take your punishment, baby?"

I nodded as dread filled me.

"It's not going to be pleasant. You've been a real brat lately."

"Yes, Sir. I understand."

"Ten strokes with the cane then."

Fuck. Oh god. I cursed a blue streak as the evil rattan cane screamed through the air and laid a strip of fire across the back of my thighs. Sir took pity on me and did a quick ten stripes up my thighs and over my ass. A solid block of burning pain, then it was over.

Tears blurred my vision as the pain flooded into pleasure. Sir's zipper rasped, his jeans crinkled and then his naked body pressed against mine. Hot skin against my welts added a layer to my punishment. "What a good girl, taking your punishment so well. Are you ready for your reward?" His cock slipped between my legs and rubbed across my labia, bumped my clit.

"Yes, Sir!" I tugged at my cuffs, knowing he was too tall, and I too short, to really do anything in this position.

He gave in to my body's pleading and unhooked me from the cross, then took me over to the huge four-poster bed that dominated the room. A minute later, he returned with Sasha, quivering, pupils blown. She looked irresistible.

Next to me on the bed, Sasha pulled me down to her mouth and our lips fused in a hot kiss. In her subspace babble, she whispered, "Please let me stay, Mistress. I'll be so good. Let me stay with you and Sir."

My heart warmed, and I smiled against her lips. "Yes, honey. You're not going anywhere." Sir interrupted and kissed her, then me.

In a tangle of limbs and mouths and hearts, I chased the deep contentment that had eluded me for too long, at last falling into a deep sleep surrounded by the man who owned my submission and the woman who freed me enough to give it.

WHAT HAPPENS
IN DENVER

Cheyenne Blue

When she thinks back, the evening is like the fragmented memory of inebriation. Not the gut-wrenching upchuck of excess tequila, but the hazy, floating dreamscape of too much champagne. There's a drifting, gauzy quality to it, an evening viewed through a lace curtain, or the ground as seen from a plane. You know it's there; you know you're connected to it, but it all seems so far away. Unreal.

Sometimes she chants the patterns in her head as she sits at her desk and covertly watches the others. Gina fucked Drew. Paul fucked Gina. And Paul fucked Drew. When she uses *fucked*, with its harsh, abrupt, guttural sound, the evening becomes something it wasn't at the time: it becomes a mishmash of body parts, of cocks and cunts, with no minds, no feelings. The ethereal dreamscape (accompanied in her remembering by a delicate symphony of strings, filmed through a forgiving cloudy lens) is laid bare, the edges sharp and clear cut.

She watches the others watch each other. Sometimes she

sees them watching her in that way, but their eyes always slide away, back to the computer screen, so that there is no accidental connection. It's an evening that never was, now unacknowledged. So she goes back to staring glassy-eyed at her own computer, not seeing the columns of numbers lined up neatly on her screen, instead seeing Drew's bulky golden body over hers, feeling the slide of his fat cock inside her, seeing Paul's lean darkly furred body alongside her, his lips meeting Drew's.

"So boring." Drew flung himself into the chair opposite hers. "Weather delay. They're saying we won't get out until morning. Paul's trying to get us rooms." He gestured at the other man, pacing the crowded departure area, cell phone glued to his ear. Above his head, the board flashed red with delays and cancellations.

Gina closed her laptop. "I've heard many of the roads are impassible. I hope he can get rooms close by. The worst thing about Denver is how far the airport is from anything—"

"Anything interesting." Drew rolled his eyes. "No doubt he'll get rooms close by and we'll be staring at each other over a faceless hotel bar."

"Move it." Paul reappeared. "They're holding rooms for us, but they'll only keep them for twenty minutes. Lots of folks stranded." Without waiting to check whether they were following, he set off briskly to the terminal exit.

Gina trotted in his wake with Drew, their luggage wheels clacking briskly over the tiled floor. Outside the terminal, the snow blew horizontally, stinging her cheeks even underneath the canopy. Somehow Paul already had a taxi, his bag in the trunk, himself in the front seat gesticulating to the driver. Gina slid into the rear seat with Drew, and the taxi pulled away, snow tires gripping the packed snow. Drew shifted restlessly beside her, his fine woolen suit pulling tight over heavy thighs. Gina watched his hands, clenching and unclenching on his leg. Fine hands for such a solid man. Long fingers. Attractive fingers. Drew seemed agitated. Eager to get home no doubt. She wondered if he had a lover back in Indianapolis.

The hotel foyer was busy, but Paul shouldered his way to the desk, and returned in a few minutes.

"Third floor," he said.

Paul found room 303 and opened the door. Light spilled across the counterpanes of the two queen beds, eerily harsh from reflected snow. "There's a problem," he said. "This is our room."

Gina looked around. It was the usual clean but nondescript hotel room she stayed in all the time. Bright counterpane over white duvet cover. Standard wooden desk with lamp and hotel information laid out in soldier rows underneath the mirror. Flat-screen TV aimed somewhere between the two beds.

"It looks fine," she said.

Paul smiled slightly. "I think you missed the emphasis," he said. "This is *our* room. One room for all three of us. It's the last room."

She didn't want to look at either of them. Bad enough that she had to share a room with colleagues, but if there were winks or swiftly hidden smiles it would make things worse. A drink after a conference was one thing; this was another level, another rise in the slope to intimacy. There was a flash in her head of Drew's long fingers tapping patterns on his leg during the taxi ride. If it had been the two of them, alone in this hotel room... She suppressed a smile.

When she glanced back at them, their expressions were blank. It gave her confidence. "We'll manage," she said briskly. "Is there a pullout bed?"

Paul's expression eased slightly in the face of her breezy acceptance. "No. They're already taken."

"Then we'll toss for the floor." Digging in her bag, she produced three quarters. "Odd one out gets the floor."

Gina and Paul tossed heads, and Drew tails. He pulled a face. "I'll live."

Movement gave her a focus. She checked the wardrobe, pulling out spare pillows in plastic wrap and two blankets.

Drew regarded her gloomily, then switched his gaze to Paul. "You better spring for a decent dinner, boss."

The hotel bar was crowded, not only with guests, but with many travelers and their luggage. Paul found them seats at the bar, and pulled over the menu. "I suggest we get our order in; they're bound to be busy."

His words were prophetic. Three glasses of wine later, and Gina's world took on a muted ethereal quality. Her colleagues were sharp-focused against a background of pattern and color. She could have been anywhere; the edges of her reality stopped at their corner of the bar. When the food finally arrived, she found she wasn't hungry, and merely picked at the assortment of chicken wings and other fried snacks. She sipped on another glass of wine and watched the men gnaw on the chicken, dunk fries into catsup. But the conversation ran free, and she matched their tall tales with her own. Some were even true.

When they finally made it back to their room, all she wanted was to get her head on the pillow and sleep. The wine made her head spin, and she tucked a hand in the crook of each of their arms and let them lead her in. She claimed the bathroom and emerged soon after in the long T-shirt she slept in. Ignoring Drew's mutterings about the floor, she slipped into the far bed and turned her back to sleep.

When she woke, an hour or a few later, the moonlight shone

through the window that none of them had bothered to cover with the drapes. The silver light illuminated the room, softening its austere look, turning edges to shining silver. The room overlooked the freeway, eerily deserted in the moonlight, the snow falling softly blurring the edges between dream and reality. There was little sound; merely the distant hum of heating. And then Gina heard the soft intake of breath, the rustle of sheets in the next bed. She lay quiet on her back, eyes open into the silver air. A murmur, the slow drag of sheet over skin, a gentle creak as someone shifted position. Carefully, she turned her head to the left. There in the next bed, Drew and Paul lay together, their lower bodies underneath the sheet, their arms entwined. Kissing, their lips meshing, blending, then parting for a breath, before returning to sup at each other's mouths. Their upper bodies gleamed with starlight, highlighting the contrast between sharp fingers and bulky curved muscle. With a rustle of sheet, Drew moved over on top of Paul and bent his head to taste again.

Her short intake of breath sounded loud in the room. Gina closed her eyes, wishing she could take back the sound. They were so beautiful. Their bodies melding, Drew's golden furred body against Paul's leaner, darker one. But the men had frozen at the sound. The room hung poised in the moonlight, a tableau of spiraling passion etched in the silver light.

Gina swallowed, and her mouth opened to say, "Sorry," or "Please do carry on," or "Don't mind me," and she gripped the sheet, prepared to turn her back to them, to give them what privacy she could, when Paul stretched out a hand, over the space between the two beds.

"Join us," he said.

She could have said no. It would have been easier to smile, turn away, even to leave the room and sleep on a couch in the bar with other travelers. But her hesitation gave the men confidence.

Drew raised up from Paul and fixed her in his gaze. "Join us," he said in echo of Paul.

Gina sat up, swung her legs over the side of the bed, stood and walked the pace to the other bed, slipping her T-shirt up and over her head as she went. Drew flipped the sheet away from their bodies, moved away from Paul, so that she saw them clearly, the way their erections strained.

She wasn't sure which of them grasped her hand, pulled her down to them, but then she was in the middle, and Paul was kissing her, his mouth warm and wet, and yes, salty with a familiar taste. She reached down, palmed his smooth cock, rubbed a thumb over the moisture she found at the tip.

Behind her, Drew spooned in close, his erection nestled against her bottom. One hand curved around and circled a nipple with a gentle touch, a soft touch for such a big man. Any half-formed thoughts about being a third wheel, only good to suck on the spare cock, flew out into the clear night. For Paul kissed her with intent, almost with reverence, with light, butterfly lips. Drew's hand roamed a sure pathway along her side, stroking over her hip, to rest on her bush. The patterns he'd tapped on his thigh in the taxi now played with excruciating slowness between her thighs.

Gina raised her leg to allow him better access, and his fingers slipped between, questing through her folds, spreading the moisture he found, rubbing around her clit like a pearl.

Paul's lips left her mouth and started a long, winding quest down her body. She watched his dark head through half-closed eyes, as her mind floated free in the moonlight, still relaxed from the wine. Paul's mouth closed over a nipple, and he sucked in gentle counterpoint to the rubbing of Drew's fingers between her legs.

Drew's cock nudged lower, brushing her folds.

"May I, Gina?" he breathed into her ear.

In answer, she raised her thigh higher, and his tip dipped inside her. Drew's fingers left her clit to grip her hip, and he pushed farther into her pussy. The pleasure was intense, powerful and oh-so-right. Gina forgot that they were workmates. Instead, they were simply bodies, aligned in pleasure, giving and receiving, with her as the centerpiece, the axis of their pleasure.

Paul moved up and across Gina, so that his lips could meet Drew's. The men kissed, a slow to and fro, in time with the easy thrusts of Drew's cock in Gina's pussy. Paul's cock bobbed in front of her, too far away to take into her mouth, so she settled for palming it, a steady caress, feeling her boss swell under her hand.

She would come, she knew, and soon, the combination of cock and skin and visual bringing an intensity to the encounter. She wasn't rushing, didn't want to force the moment, but when Drew slid his hand down between her legs again, there was no holding back and she came in shuddering rushes, her cunt muscles fluttering around Drew's cock, shivering under his fingers.

The men broke the kiss. The sheet that had previously covered them was gone, pooled on the floor in a drift of cream. Paul moved, reversed his position, and curled around on the bed. Gina realized why, as he maneuvered his hips so that his thick cock was within reach of her lips. Bobbing forward, she tasted him, in quick, tiny licks, until he groaned and pushed his hips even closer, his length nudging her mouth until she sucked him deep inside.

Behind her, Drew increased his strokes so that he was stroking firmly in and out. Gina closed her eyes, concentrated on sucking

Paul's cock, on the fullness of fucking down below. When she thought there could be no greater pleasure, Paul moved again. Hot breath fanned over her pussy, and then she felt his tongue exploring where she and Drew joined. Wet and hot, he licked her, around her pussy, over her clit, passing over her lips, and then lower.

"Christ," Drew muttered. "That's incredible."

His cock stilled inside her and she realized that Paul must be licking his cock where it was embedded in her. His tongue flickered around, away and back. Drew swelled inside her, and even in his stillness she realized he was teetering on the edge. She redoubled her sucking of Paul's cock, the images in her head of what she couldn't see down below pushing her own pleasure up to new heights.

She wasn't sure who was going to come first, but then Drew's breath hitched in his throat, and his cock withdrew and thrust, once, convulsively, and he poured his heat inside her. His face dropped to her neck, his breathing ragged in her ear. Moisture—his and hers—coated her thighs.

Gina swirled her tongue over Paul's cock, wanting him to have a share in the pleasure. His answering groan and the undulation of his hips told her he had no complaints. A taste of salt, and she reached for his balls with her fingers, finding them up tight and hard against his body. Another few seconds and he blew into her mouth, in a rush of salt and passion.

It wasn't over. Even as Gina relaxed, Drew's hand once again tightened on her hip. He was still half-hard, she realized, buried within her. And Paul's head was still between her thighs. His mouth touched again on her cunt, and this time his lips and tongue worked her clit, tiny circles of joy, spiraling out from her center, until her whole body was aflame. She clenched down on Drew's cock, and the world exploded into heat and light, golden and jeweled behind her eyes, her world focused on fingers and tongues and cocks and cunts and all the combinations she could imagine.

They slept that night in one bed. Gina, the touchstone, in the middle, on her back, with Drew and Paul on either side. The men faced her, Drew's heavy thigh over her own, Paul's long fingers on her breast. And at some point in the night, there was more kissing, and caresses that led to a second hazy coupling, and this time Paul fucked both Drew and Gina before adding his spend to Drew's in Gina's pussy. Gina sucked both men, and both men used lips and tongues and fingers to draw an explosive response from her. In the moonlight, they were all beautiful, all creatures of light and air.

DIA was operating again the next morning, and the backlog of flights was reduced enough by early afternoon that they were able to secure a flight to Indianapolis.

Gina stared ahead, at the back of Drew's head as they checked in. Paul was back to boss mode, organizing taxis, on the phone to the office.

Did it really happen? wondered Gina. *Did it, did I, did they?*

They had a row of three seats on the plane, and they sat, each pretending to be engrossed in their laptops and reports. Gina was in the middle. *Just like last night,* she thought.

After the coffee service, Paul turned to the other two. "About last night," he said, and there was a diffidence in his gaze, a nervousness in the way his fingers clutched the paper cup. "It was...amazing. One of the most incredible nights of my life." He stretched a hand toward Gina, and she took it, wrapping her fingers around his. On her other side, Drew took her hand, interlacing their fingers tightly.

"It can't happen again," Paul continued. "What happens in Denver, stays in Denver."

Gina nodded. She knew this. Indeed, this formal acknowledgment of what they were to each other was more than she expected.

"I'd like to continue this," said Paul. "But I can't. I'm your boss. It's not right. I could be seen to be taking advantage of you. Both of you."

On her other side, Drew snorted softly.

"You two though..." Paul drew a deep breath. "There's nothing to prevent you seeing each other."

With a nod, he rose, left his report on his seat and made his way to the restrooms at the rear of the plane.

Gina looked at Drew. He quirked a smile at her. "Shall we?" he asked.

"I'd like that."

Paul walks past Gina's desk with a brief, professional nod, his eyes sliding away from deeper contact.

I remember, she thinks. *I will never forget.*

It's five o'clock, so she rises, takes her jacket from the back of her chair, calls a general good-bye to her colleagues and swings out toward the street. Drew meets her at the door, proffering an arm. She reaches up, presses a kiss to his cheek.

"How about Vietnamese takeout for dinner tonight?" he asks.

"You always say that when it's your turn to cook," she says, and linking her arm with his, they step out onto the crowded street.

OLD HABITS

Mina Murray

When I told my boyfriend, Luke, that Alyx would be staying with me over the holiday weekend, he went silent for a while.

"Are you sure that's a good idea?" he finally asked, quietly. "You know, considering how things ended?"

How things ended was...badly. Very badly. I hadn't spoken to Alyx for years. It was only by chance that I'd run into her a month ago, when we were both in the city on business. It was one of those fluke things, where you take a certain path, a different path from the one you normally would, and it changes things.

To be honest, I hadn't recognized her until *after* she'd bumped into me, quite literally, outside the bar on Fifteenth Street. I could hardly be blamed, though. She looked totally different from the person I remembered. The punk goddess look she had favored in college—the safety-pin piercings, torn T-shirts and Doc Martens—was gone, replaced by an impeccably tailored dress, a cherry-red trench coat and killer heels that gave her those extra inches of height she had always wanted. Gone, too, was the peroxide-blonde pixie crop. Her hair had reverted to its natural color—a rich chocolate brown—and was artfully layered around her heart-shaped face. Without the heavy black eyeliner she used to wear, her eyes positively shone. I had forgotten how unusual they were, a shade of hazel flecked with gold and green. Beautiful. Stunning.

I would like to think that if I had recognized her, I would have spoken first. Been the bigger person. But I don't know if that would have been true. At any rate, it's not like I had the chance to test the theory.

"Eve?" she asked, "Eve, is that you?"

I could have pretended not to hear her. I could have flat-out ignored her. There was something in her tone, though, something tentative and wistful, that resonated with me, in some long-forgotten way. So I stopped, and I said hello, and I kissed her on the cheek. We stood there for some time, on the sidewalk in the late autumn air, mapping out for each other the divergent paths our lives had taken and who of the old crowd we'd kept in touch with.

Before long the wind picked up and I shivered.

"Well, it was great running into you, Alyx, but I should get going before I freeze."

"Are you sure you don't have time for a drink?" she asked.

She put her hand on my arm and turned those big hazel eyes on me. Those eyes that had talked me into so many things in the past.

I made a show of checking my watch, even though I knew I had nowhere to be. *One drink*, I told myself, *just one. What's the harm?* We were right outside a bar, after all. It would have been rude to refuse.

It was crowded inside, of course. Full of Friday afternoon

regulars and others seeking respite from the weather, some liquid fortification before the long commute home.

"Quick," Alyx exclaimed, "let's grab those seats there, before anyone else gets them."

She gripped my hand and tugged me across the room. She had always liked taking the lead. Some things never changed.

"Brilliant," she said, as we settled onto our bar stools. "Now for those drinks."

Liquor is a great icebreaker, but still...I was surprised at how easily Alyx and I fell back into our old rhythms. One drink turned into two, and then three, and then we started reminiscing about some of the dumber stunts we had pulled in college.

"Do you remember that time you nearly got kicked out?"

"Ugh," I said, "don't remind me. It was your fault, though."

"Hey," Alyx protested, "don't blame me. I made *one* suggestion about streaking. You didn't have to actually do it."

"You called me a chicken! Of course I had to do it!"

"I was just the excuse you needed." She waved her hand dismissively. "Besides, you would've got away with it. It's not my fault you wanted a naked photo in the dean's office."

"How was I supposed to know he was screwing his assistant after hours?"

"Just as well he was with her and not alone." Alyx took a sip of her cocktail, her pink tongue darting out to lick the sugar-frosted rim. Some of the crystals stuck to her lipsticked mouth. She brushed them off with her fingertips, paused for a moment, then licked them too. She caught me watching and a slow grin spread across her face. "The only thing that saved your sweet ass was the threat of his wife finding out."

Alyx shimmied around, so we were facing each other. She was about to say something when she gave a slight jolt and her eyes widened.

"Oh!" she said, and clapped a hand over her mouth.

"What?"

"My suspender strap just pinged loose."

"So go to the bathroom and fix it."

"I can't," she said, with a giggle. "What if the other one goes too and my stocking falls down?"

"Well—"

"It's fine, I'll do it here. Should only take a sec."

Instead of swinging back around, as I'd expected—which would have concealed what she was about to do—Alyx rested her feet on the rungs of my bar stool. My right leg was now trapped between hers.

With eyes downcast, and palms flat against her thighs, she inched her dress slowly upward. Tightly woven fishnet gave way to fine lace, and then to bare flesh. Sure enough, the strap dangled indolently against her thigh. The clip itself was the old-fashioned metal kind, with teeth that should have gripped the silky fabric firmly enough to prevent such mishaps.

She reached down and secured the offending strap, pinching the stocking taut between her red-varnished fingernails. I couldn't help but notice that her legs were shapelier than they used to be. It suited her.

"There," she said brightly. "All done!"

Well, not entirely. She had forgotten—neglected?—to smooth her dress back down. When she made no move to do so, I reached out and did it for her.

She was starting to thank me when I heard a man curse. The waiter bearing our dinner, distracted by something, had tripped over his shoes and was lurching toward us.

Alyx managed to snatch the platter from his hands, a second before he landed with a thud at her feet.

"Well, hello there," she smiled, utterly nonplussed, as if men prostrated themselves before her on a daily basis.

"Bon appétit," he groaned.

The rest of the evening passed uneventfully, and soon we were standing on the sidewalk again, saying our good-byes. We'd exchanged details already, back at the bar, but before I knew it, I was inviting her to visit. I had promised myself that I would stay on guard, but Alyx had charmed me in spite of myself. Plus, alcohol tended to make me generous, sometimes to a fault.

Over the next few weeks, I thought seriously about making up some excuse so I could back out of my offer. As much fun as I'd had that night, our history was complicated. Every time I actually sat down to write the email, though, I remembered something urgent I had to do instead.

So here she was, sitting cross-legged on my couch, cradling a cup of spiked hot chocolate to ward off the winter chill.

"This place is gorgeous," Alyx said. "And it's so restful out here."

"It suits me," I shrugged. "I work from home a lot, so I like the peace and quiet. It isn't fancy, but I have everything I need."

I was pleased she'd commented on the house. It was my pride and joy. I had gone to a lot of trouble to decorate it, to find that balance between rustic and modern, earthy and feminine.

I joined her on the couch, curling my feet up underneath me.

"You should have made some chocolate for yourself," she said. "Here, have some of mine."

She didn't so much pass her cup to me as hold it to my lips and tilt it so I could drink. With our height difference, it was hardly a surprise when a few drops got away from her and spilled over my chin.

"Oops, sorry," Alyx giggled. "Let me get that."

She reached for me, then, brushing her fingers up over my chin, past the little indentation beneath my bottom lip. Her fingertips pressed against my mouth, which parted for her just as willingly as it used to. A familiar pulse began to beat between my legs. Sense memory.

The doorbell rang then, and thank god it did, because otherwise I might have done something really stupid.

When I opened the door, Luke was stamping his feet against the cold, the heavy soles of his boots scraping against the welcome mat.

"Ma'am," he winked.

He bent down to kiss me, bringing with him a rush of cold smoky air. His lips were like ice against mine. But they soon thawed when he deepened our kiss and slid his tongue into my mouth. When he pulled away from me, I was sure that I was blushing. I'd forgotten for a minute that we had an audience. I stepped aside to let him in.

Alyx watched him intently, tracking his every step as he hung up his coat and crossed the room.

Luke tends to have that effect on people. Tall, broad shouldered, with black hair and blue eyes and those white, white teeth. He makes it hard not to stare. The tight jeans don't hurt either.

He walked right over to Alyx and introduced himself. She didn't bother getting up, just flashed him her brilliant smile and took his hand without a word. When they touched, I felt an odd twang, as if something had sprung loose inside me. I shut the door and joined them.

After dinner, we sat on the floor in the living room, talking about not very much. Luke knelt in front of the fireplace to arrange the logs he'd split for me earlier in the week and in no

time at all there was a healthy blaze going. The quiet was punc-
tuated with the crackling of wood. We opened a fine bottle
of red, something I'd been saving for a special occasion, and
toasted each other. The wine lulled us, and the fire warmed us,
and outside it started raining, heavy droplets beating against
the windowpanes, drumming against the roof.

As the hours went by, we finished that first bottle, and then
another. It was halfway through the third when things started
to unravel. The drunker Alyx got, the more she flirted with
Luke, until she was practically throwing herself at him right in
front of me. He did nothing to encourage her, of course, and
tried to put a damper on her behavior by being more overtly
affectionate toward me. But that just seemed to make things
worse. She bristled whenever he put his hand on my leg.

Eventually I'd had enough.

"It's time we called it a night," I said and stood, abruptly.
"Alyx, I'll show you to the guest room."

She struggled to get to her feet, bumping against one of the
side tables and nearly knocking over a stained-glass lamp. I
reached out to steady her, but she shrugged me off.

"I can manage."

"Fine. End of the hall, on your left. Towels are—"

She stormed off before I'd had a chance to finish speaking, and
I wondered how the evening had gone so wrong, so quickly.

"Well, that was weird," Luke said when we got back to my
bedroom.

"Not weird," I spat. "Just Alyx."

I didn't know why I had assumed she'd changed. I should
never have invited her back into my life.

I flung open the wardrobe doors and grabbed my sleep shorts,
then switched on the gas heater that lined the wall. The room

was frigid. Cold radiated from the windowpanes, condensation collecting on the inside of the glass.

Luke sat on the end of the bed, his expression thoughtful.

"She really didn't like me touching you, you know. Is there something you haven't told me?"

I hesitated.

"It's nothing, really."

Luke raised an eyebrow.

"Just a little college experimentation. Two girls having fun, whenever we were between boyfriends. For Alyx, that was every couple of months." I snorted. "She never could hold on to a guy for more than a few weeks. Probably explains why she was always hitting on mine."

The room had warmed up a little, enough for me to start undressing. Luke watched as I tossed my sweater onto the armchair in the corner of the room.

"Need a hand?"

I was angry at the way things had gone, but that was no reason to deny myself the pleasure of Luke's touch.

"Sure," I whispered.

He shot me that look of his, that smoldering look that never failed to hit me right between my legs, then beckoned me over.

Still sitting on the bed, he unbuttoned my shirt maddeningly slowly, pressing kisses to each inch of revealed skin. When the fabric hit the ground, he reached out and in one swift movement flicked open the front clasp of my bra.

"Yeah," he breathed, palming my breasts, "better."

He didn't tease anymore then, just stripped my jeans and panties from me ruthlessly and tumbled me onto the bed.

"Fast or slow, babe?" he asked, shucking his clothes. The sound of his belt clanking on the floorboards sent a pulse of need through me.

"Fast, please."

I groaned when he wriggled down the bed to get at my pussy. Fast meant he would get me wet, get me ready for him. But fast also meant that he wouldn't make me come with his mouth, and that was fine by me tonight.

He licked my clit, once, twice; slid a finger inside me.

"Jesus, babe, you're wet."

I couldn't deny it. My body had been buzzing all night. Maybe from the wine, maybe something else. Whatever it was, I needed Luke, and now. No foreplay, no preliminaries.

"I'm on top," I growled.

The bliss I felt sinking onto his length was incredible. He was hot and hard and perfect, just perfect. My cunt clenched around him in welcome.

I leaned down to press my lips to his, sucking his tongue into my mouth. His moan vibrated low in my body. I undulated to drive him deeper, slammed my palms down on his shoulders. Leverage.

"So good," I crooned.

Luke let me set the pace. But that didn't stop him grabbing my ass with those big hands of his and thrusting up to meet me. His fingers soon strayed across my flesh, between my buttocks, finding the tightness of my asshole.

There was a question in his eyes.

I bit my lip and nodded.

When he pushed his finger inside me, I swear that I saw stars. That forbidden friction, the way his cock stroked over my G-spot, the way the root of him brushed against my clit, set off sparklers throughout my body.

"Come with me, babe," Luke urged.

And I did. I cried out my pleasure into the silent night, wondering the whole time I was coming if Alyx could hear me, down the hall.

We spooned for a while, until Luke fell asleep. My body was sated, and I knew I was physically tired enough, but I just couldn't drift off the way I usually did. I lay there for a half hour, before I figured a shower might help.

When I got out of the bathroom, the door across the hall opened, and Alyx ducked her head out.

I stared at her coldly.

"Eve, can I talk to you for a minute?"

"I'm tired. Whatever you have to say to me can wait until morning."

The door opened a bit wider.

"It's just...I just wanted to apologize."

"Then you can do it in the morning."

Footsteps followed me, all the way to my bedroom door.

"Eve, please!"

I turned with a sigh and was surprised by what I saw. Alyx looked contrite. Genuinely contrite. Not at all the crocodile-tears expression she used to wear when trying to talk herself out of a jam.

"I should never have come here. I was an idiot to think that things could be different. Not after everything that happened, not after..." She shook her head.

But I wasn't letting her off that easy.

"Not after I caught you, you mean? Fucking *my* boyfriend, in *my* bed?"

She nodded, miserable.

"Do you have any idea how much you hurt me? How long it took me to get over that? You were my best friend. I loved you."

"Not the way I loved you." She lifted her eyes to mine. "It was never about the guys, Eve. It was always about you. I wanted it to be just us, just you and me. I wanted to prove that none of those guys deserved you. But then I didn't deserve you either. I just didn't see it at the time."

She took in a shaky breath.

"So I wanted to say sorry, for then and especially for tonight. I insulted your hospitality, I offended your boyfriend and I acted like a fool."

I wasn't sure what to say to her. Everyone has those imaginary conversations in her head, where she rehashes old conflicts, tries to work through them. But I never imagined ours going like this, with me barefoot and in a bathrobe, hair dripping wet, my boyfriend snoring in the room behind me.

"I'll be gone in the morning, don't worry," Alyx said. "I just wanted to say good-bye first."

I could think of a hundred good reasons for why what I was about to do was a terrible idea. But when I kissed her, swallowing her sound of surprise, none of them seemed to matter. Nothing mattered except the lushness of her body, pressed up against me, and the way her perfume filled my senses. Nothing mattered except the way she kissed me back, desperate and fierce and tender. She was crying, I could tell. Or maybe that was me.

After a few intense moments, my head was spinning, and I had to break the kiss. I took her face in my hands and leaned in close.

"You're not going anywhere," I said. "Understand?"

"Can I...can I kiss you again?" she asked, as if she had to, as if she didn't know what rights she had over my body.

"Please."

Her fingers traced the column of my neck. I guess I should have been more specific when I granted her request, because she slipped the robe off my shoulder, baring one breast, and pressed a wet kiss to my nipple.

She may as well have kissed my clit, the effect was so elec-trifying.

"Oh god," I murmured, as she drew the tight peak into her mouth and bit gently.

Her hand found the cord of my robe and tugged it loose. The satiny garment practically fell off me then, leaving me naked in front of her.

I wasn't normally like this, so passive, so acquiescent. But I didn't resist when she placed her small hand flat against my breastbone and pushed me into the bedroom.

"I've missed the way you come under my tongue," she whispered.

I don't know how she could see so well in the dark, but she managed to get us into the room without any noise, and without me tripping over something. An impressive feat, considering I was lust-dazed, walking backward, and clumsy at the best of times.

She moved me to the foot of the bed and gently pushed me onto my back. My head was cushioned on the mattress, my body on the blanket box, my legs draped over her shoulders.

And then she put her mouth on me, and I almost wept. I had forgotten what it was like to be with a woman, but Alyx reminded me with her slim fingers, her soft skin, her long hair brushing silkily along the inside of my thighs. It was hard not to whimper when she tongued my bud delicately; harder still to bite back the moan when she captured it between her lips and sucked.

That Luke was sleeping not two feet away from me only made me more aroused. I shut my eyes as Alyx flattened her tongue and swept it over me. It felt like she was everywhere at once.

Something brushed against my cheek all of a sudden, and I

nearly jumped out of my skin. Luke was watching me.

I swallowed, hard.

"Um, Alyx..." I said.

She didn't look up, though she did take her mouth off me for a moment.

"Eve," she whispered furiously, "if you can talk while I'm doing this, I've seriously lost my touch."

"You have to stop," I said, urgently. "We, um, have an audience."

Luke switched on the reading lamp, momentarily blinding us all. I wish it had lasted. The darkness made things less real.

Alyx had the grace to look embarrassed when Luke extended his hand in a parody of greeting.

"Hello. Remember me? I'm the boyfriend."

Well, shit. I had no idea what to do next, never having been dumb enough to get myself into a scrape like this before.

But Luke had always been good at thinking on his feet. When Alyx held out her hand, he pulled it to his chest, dragging her onto the bed, and sucked her index and middle fingers into his mouth. The same fingers that had been inside me only moments before.

"Oh *fuck*," I said, craning my neck to get a better view.

I stared, entranced, as Luke's tongue flickered between her fingers. I knew the gesture was meant to mock, to lewdly simulate the act he'd caught us in, but I didn't care. I was too unbearably turned on, seeing him steal the taste of me from her.

When Luke finally relinquished her hand, Alyx was breathing hard, spots of color flushing her pretty cheeks. There may have been an additional reason for that. Now that we had some light, Luke's position on our situation was very clear.

He was harder than I had ever seen him before.

Well, that's a good sign, I thought.

"Now," he said, "seeing as you both woke me up, I think I deserve some compensation." He looked down at his erection. "Which one of you is going to blow me first?"

I was now officially so far out at sea that I couldn't even see the shore. So I did the only thing I could think of under the circumstances, and reached for my boyfriend's cock.

"Don't you have any manners, Eve?" Alyx said, throwing a sultry glance at Luke. "I'm the guest. You should have asked if I wanted to go first."

A spark leapt between my boyfriend and my former best friend, and I wasn't sure whether to be pleased or terrified. The thought of them *both* ganging up on me left me weak at the knees.

"Apologize to your friend, honey," Luke encouraged. "Actually, better yet, undress her."

That, I could do. I made short work of it, too. Tossing aside her sweater. Peeling off her trousers. Tearing the lacy underwear from her body. She kneeled on the mattress, her figure glorious in the golden light. I dove between her legs, greedy for the taste of her. She cried out at once and doubled over.

When Luke's hand connected with my ass, the noise echoed all around the room. I looked up at him in shock.

"I said undress her, not maul her." He turned to Alyx. "I do apologize."

"No problem," she gasped, as I gave her clit one last kiss.

"Now, where were we...?" Luke tapped his chin. "Oh that's right," he said, pointing at Alyx. "You were going to go down on me. Eve, honey, be a sweetheart and come hold your friend's hair back? I want to see all of this."

Alyx and I crawled over to where Luke was kneeling. He'd positioned himself at the top of the bed, so he could sit back against the wall if he needed to.

Alyx moistened her lips and leaned forward. Slowly but surely, inch by inch, my boyfriend's prick disappeared into her beautiful mouth. I couldn't believe this was happening.

Luke threw his head back and groaned.

Feelings assailed me faster than I could name them. As soon as I'd identified one, I was hit with another. Jealousy. Greed. Love. Desire. Rage. Indignation, too, though I knew I had no right to be feeling that. Had I been trying to rewrite the past when I'd invited Luke over? It struck me now that maybe I had. What other reason could I have named for inviting my current boyfriend to dinner with the woman who had always tried to seduce my boyfriends before? Whatever my motivation, it had turned out okay. At least this time I was *enjoying* seeing my boyfriend and my best friend fuck.

But that didn't mean I wasn't competitive. I pulled Alyx away from Luke's cock and started blowing him myself, determined to go deeper than she had, even if I choked in the process.

"Fuck, Eve. Oh my *god* that's so good," Luke cried.

Alyx bit her way up Luke's torso, then silenced him with a kiss. He responded hungrily, threading one hand through her hair and pressing the other between her legs. I kept my eyes open the whole time, watching as he plunged two fingers deep inside her, and circled her clit with his thumb. Alyx and I both moaned in tandem. I knew exactly what she was feeling, knew how fucking good Luke was with his hands. I was jealous of her and pleased for her at the same time.

Even though it had been years, I remembered the way Alyx looked when she was about to come. The crimson flush that crept over her neck, the way her thigh muscles quivered, the throaty little moans that got louder and louder, until her climax hit. I watched as she broke apart in my boyfriend's arms, sobbing with relief.

He held her until she calmed, then gathered her into the crook of his arm. He does afterglow well, my Luke. That doesn't mean he's entirely selfless, though. His eyes narrowed, as if he'd just realized my lips weren't wrapped around him.

His expression turned steely, and god help me, I loved it.

"Climb onto my cock, Eve," he ordered. "No, the other way, so I can stare at your ass."

Luke kept his arm around Alyx, who gave no indication she planned on moving. She did let me hold her hand, though, for balance. For the second time that night, I sank onto Luke's cock, welcoming him into my body. I don't think I'd ever loved him more.

His long legs were stretched out in front of him, toes curling in pleasure. I had a feeling he wouldn't last long this time, not after all this excitement.

Alyx murmured something in his ear, but I couldn't hear what it was. I was too lost in the slide of Luke's cock inside me, in the way he gripped my neck, in the sudden feel of...soft flesh pressing against me. My eyes snapped open.

Alyx must have asked Luke's permission to move. Because there she was in front of me. So close I could see my own reflection in her eyes.

"Luke said this was okay."

"You actually asked first?" I panted. "Who are you, and what have you done with my friend?"

She kissed me then, and on her mouth I tasted us all, me and her and Luke. A reminder of the way we'd shared ourselves tonight.

The way she tweaked my nipples as she kissed me would have been painful if I hadn't been so far gone. Sliding down my body in her old familiar way, she found that place where Luke and I were joined, and when she kissed us there it felt like something both sacred and profane.

Luke had his hands on my hips now, controlling my rhythm. Whenever he lifted me off him, Alyx laved his shaft with her tongue. Whenever he dropped me onto him, Alyx loved my clit with her lips. It didn't take long before I started to shake, and I had to wind my arms back, around Luke's neck, to stay upright. When my moment of joy came, it was like nothing I'd ever felt before. It was like my whole body was made of light. Intense spasms wracked me as I came, my body tightening around one lover, and trembling under the other's tongue. I dimly heard Luke's groans as he shuddered through his own orgasm. I hoped he'd experienced what I had.

Alyx was gentle when she helped me off Luke. She stayed for a little bit, until we came back to ourselves. Then she kissed us both and started toward the door.

"Don't be silly," said Luke, drowsily. "The bed's big enough for three."

So Alyx and I nestled down on either side of him, holding hands over his body. Sleep took the two of them quickly, but passed me over. This time I didn't mind. It gave me a chance to think about what had happened tonight. Where it left us—me and Alyx, me and Luke—I didn't know. I guessed we'd just have to muddle through it as we went along, like everyone does with that thing called life.

MEDLEY
OF DESIRE

A. J. Lyle

'm driving myself crazy. Little by little, day by day, one thought at a time, I'm forming an endless chasm in my heart that I'm pretty sure will eventually tear me apart, force me to choose, when all I want is for my fantasies to become my reality.

The chirping of the crosswalk signal drifts through my mind, and I move forward with the crowd. I'm walking. I don't know where to yet, and I don't really care, I just know I need to figure this shit out—now.

After a quick glance at the street sign to make sure I'm not heading into an unsafe area of the city or back toward the apartment building like I often do, I dedicate myself to exploring the problem from an omniscient point of view. It's harder than it sounds.

To me, it seems so simple. I've been seeing two different guys for a while now. They both know about each other and have from the beginning. They were friends far before I ever came into the picture, and they both knew what they were getting into when it all started. I never pretended to be good at monogamy, and honestly, I wouldn't try to be. Not anymore. I'm a greedy lover: my needs are varied, and I've found out the hard way that it's impossible for one man to satisfy me even fifty percent of the time. Sometimes I want soft and romantic lovemaking with all the trimmings, and other times I want to be held down and fucked hard, forced to take more than I think I can handle. It's messed up, I know, but it's part of who I am. I decided a long time ago not to think about it too hard. I couldn't care less why I am the way I am. I just am.

My guys, they accept that about me. They both know what I need and how to give it to me. The three of us often go out together, parting ways only when the sexual tension gets too high. Then, one of them takes me to bed, and the other... Hmmm. I've never really thought about what the other one does. He could sit and listen for all I know.

A chill floats up my spine at the tantalizing thought.

They've been acting strange lately. Jealous, almost. Blake has taken to glowering around like an old bull moose, and Josh has become broody and quiet. Blake's attitude isn't so surprising considering how dominating he is, but Josh...he's the optimist in our weird little relationship. He's always the one to make light of something serious without making it seem any less important, the one that keeps Blake and me both from getting mad over every little thing. The Giver.

The knowledge that these changes have to do with me has me standing on the edge of a cliff, windmilling like hell so I don't fall and become easy prey for the vultures.

I've told them both that I love them, and I've hinted and prodded my way through countless conversations, hoping that one or the other would eventually allow himself to truly think about what I've said, to see the path I've tried so hard to create for us, but it's starting to feel hopeless.

I know they've both had threesomes before, I'm almost certain they've experienced them together, and just to throw the cherry on top, I know for a fact they're both bisexual. I can't fathom why it hasn't happened yet.

Sighing, I pause my stride along with the crowd, waiting for the light to turn green. Twilight is taking over, forcing the streetlights to flicker off and on with indecision. It's time for me to head home, so I cut to the left and surge forward with a new crowd.

I'll probably see them on the way back to my apartment. Living across the hall from them guarantees that I see them several times a day, especially since they often leave their door slightly open so they'll hear me when I get home. They're both protective of me, and though sometimes it irks me how overbearing they are, deep down I love it. It makes me feel like the most important person in the world to both of them, and it empowers my fantasies ten times more than any porn I've ever seen.

With each block I walk, the crowd around me thins, and as I near our building, I catch the sound of two deep voices arguing. It's just a whisper on the wind, but my heart skips a beat and my feet speed up. I know those voices. My guys are fighting. Over me? God, I hope not.

I slam through the front of the building and rap an insistent beat on the inner doors. I don't have time to mess with digging through my bag for my keys, so I annoy the security guard, Ethan, like I sometimes do after a night out with the girls. I can never find my keys when I'm intoxicated or emotional, so I don't even try anymore.

I throw a fervent thank-you in Ethan's direction and take the stairs two at a time, scared out of my mind that I'll get there too late. I can't imagine my life without them, and the thought that they might ruin even the chance for the three of us to be friends, never mind lovers, has my guts rolling around like drunken bats have decided to take up permanent residence.

Cresting the stairs, I sprint to the end of the hall and stop dead outside their door, my gaze taking in the sight before me while my brain tries to catch up with my body.

I blink my eyes hard and fast, my conscious mind unable to interpret what I'm seeing. I look again and again; shock courses through me, but so does a frisson of sweet anticipation mixed with hope. I think back on the last two weeks in a series of flash images, and every angry word, hard look and heated argument I've witnessed starts to make total and complete sense given what I'm seeing right now.

Josh and Blake, the two men I love more than life, have fallen for each other. I can barely contain my excitement. And here I thought they were becoming jealous of each other because of me when in reality, I wasn't even a part of the animosity. I can't help but wonder how long they've held their attraction in check. Weeks? Months? Years?

Their being best friends since forever, I imagine this discovery has been a while in coming.

Relief floods me, but then, as I watch Blake's tall, muscular frame wrap around Josh's slighter, toned one, their lips locked together, tongues searching and seeking the depths of each other's mouths, I feel...conflicted. Turned on beyond all belief, without a doubt, but scared shitless and a little bit jealous too.

Hope flutters through me, whispering that my fantasies of a triad with the two men I've been in love with for months might become a reality. Absolutely. I can't recall how many times I've envisioned Blake and me double teaming Josh. He's so quiet in bed, so reserved, and I long to see him lose his control beneath the ministrations of Blake's need to dominate and my need to hear his moans and cries. And submission. I want to submit to them both at the same time. I want them to own me in every way. I want to be the center of their universes the same way they've been mine. The three of us make the perfect threesome, and the fact that maybe, just maybe, it could be based on mutual love...god, I want that so bad.

But fear finds a spot to fester. What if they don't feel the same way? What happens if they decide they want a monogamous relationship between themselves? Unlikely, perhaps, but possible. Where does that leave me? Losing both of the men I love, that's where. My breath catches in my throat as I explore the unthinkable for the umpteenth time. My fear is the only thing that has kept me from seeking out the connection I'm now witnessing between them, from asking them outright for the threesome I've so desired. Passion swarms around them like untapped energy that's always been there, waiting for release.

God, I'm scared. I know I have to come at this head-on, especially now, but I'm not so sure I can handle the heartbreak if they don't want it too.

I'm frozen in the doorway of their apartment, one hand on the doorknob, the other holding tight to the door frame for support. My gaze travels over their bodies with languid appreciation despite the turmoil of my thoughts. My heart speeds up, little by little, as I watch Blake's full lips trail along the side of Josh's neck, their hips grinding together, a groan escaping Blake's lips.

I can't keep my breath from becoming shallow, my inhalations gaining momentum with every passing second. My clit burns and throbs with the need for contact, so I let go of the doorknob and run my fingers over my jeans, pushing hard to relieve my growing arousal. I feel the slow trickle of my juices flowing down, and I can't help it, my hand reroutes, slips into the waistband of my jeans and seeks out my clit. I close my eyes and savor the rush of physical relief. But it doesn't last. Hearing Josh's needy moans, I open my eyes and watch as his hands attack the buttons of Blake's black jeans to free his hard cock. He wants him bad. Dear god, so do I.

A surge of sexual energy pierces me where I stand braced against the door frame rubbing circles around my clit. Blake's eyes meet mine and for a split second, I'm struck by the fear of rejection, but then his full lips tilt up in that sexy, wicked smile he gets when he's especially playful, and he extends his hand toward me. "Come, kitten. Be with us."

His deep voice reverberates through me, and I'm lost, drowning in a sea of longing and desire. I kick the door closed behind me and drop my bag. I know I should turn around and lock it, but I can't take my eyes off of them as they continue to stroke each other, both sets of eyes burning me with intensity and need. I never realized before how hot it is to see two men touching each other—caressing, kissing, discovering, seeking. Damn, I don't think I've ever been so turned on in my life.

I've always enjoyed gay romance, but this is something far beyond that. Instead of being forced to be the outsider while I'm reading, I've become the center of attention. My nipples harden and peak beneath my thin T-shirt, and before I can think about it, I strip it and my bra off and let them drift to the floor as I saunter forward. Blake's cock catches my attention as he rubs it against Josh, and I lick my lips in anticipation of his addictive musk coating my tongue.

I pinch and roll my nipples and moan as a jolt of electricity flies through my abdomen before branching out to encompass my entire body with a steady hum of arousal. I wonder again what it would feel like to be filled by both of them. Nothing short of heavenly, I'm sure. I get tingly just thinking about what being the center of their attentions would be like. One demanding, the other gentle, both loving.

I go to Blake first because he's the one who called me, but before my lips can find his, Josh's hands grab me and pull me tight against his chest. My breath catches as he weaves his arms through mine, trapping them behind my back and forcing me to arch my breasts upward and out. Blake doesn't waste a second before grabbing one nipple between his teeth and pinching the other between two fingers. The steady hum turns into a series of small explosions that rocket through me. I moan with the knowledge that what I'm about to experience will be life changing. I thrust my hips and grind my ass against Josh's erection while also pushing my breasts hard against Blake's mouth. He likes to tease me, though, and moves downward, trailing bites and kisses over my stomach until he reaches the waistband of my jeans.

"You're so damn responsive, kitten," Josh murmurs in my ear. "So beautiful."

With a low growl that drives me wild, Blake forces the button and zipper open and slides my pants and G-string down to my ankles in one fell swoop. My legs part without prompting, and then his wet tongue is gliding over my hood, separating my lips for his greedy mouth to claim my clit. And oh god, I've never felt anything so good. Josh holding me, his voice whispering in my ear, telling me how perfect I am for them, and Blake sucking my clit into his mouth like it's the most addictive piece of candy known to man. I shudder and shake, my breath whooshing out in sharp pants as my core tingles with the promise of release.

My heart thunders in my ears and combines with Josh's voice, pushing me to the edge. And then the scent of their combined arousals saturates my air supply and I'm lost to sensation, unable to think about anything that doesn't include my entire body riding the wild current of my fantasies coming to life.

Josh releases my arms and I drop to my knees in front of Blake and cover his thick cock with my tongue and lips, savoring the salty drop of precum at the tip before slipping my lips around him and pulling his length deep inside my mouth. The head hits the back of my throat and I feel a primal, instinctive need to feel his release pulse down my throat, filling me up with him. His hands grip my hair and hold my head still as he plunges his erection into my mouth, driving it deeper and deeper with every stroke. My scalp burns and my pussy drenches my thighs.

I feel Josh lean against me and I look up to the glorious view of their tongues intertwining, their deep moans of satisfaction filling me up with a sense of rightness I never dreamed was possible. The two men I love more than anything joined above me, lust and love combining to push us all into a timeless moment where negativity cowers before our mutual connection and ecstasy holds full domination.

"Is she going to make you come with that hot little mouth?" Josh taunts with a rasp.

I set my head at an angle so Blake can fuck my mouth and I can see everything happening above me. I don't want to miss a second of this.

Josh and Blake have their foreheads pressed together, their eyes locked. It's all I can do to finish what I started with Blake's cock. My pussy is aching, and sappy as it is, my heart yearns to be a part of that connection.

"Well?" Josh whispers. "Is she? Are you going to come in her mouth, fill her with your seed?"

Goddamn. I don't know about Blake, but Josh's comments are sending nearly painful jolts straight down to my cunt. My Kegel muscles contract, and I wonder if it really is possible to orgasm without being touched.

"Hell, yeah," Blake answers, his strained voice proving just how hard he's trying to hold himself back from doing just that.

"Tell me," Josh says huskily, "should I ask her what you taste like, or find out for myself?"

Oh hell. I can't stand this. With Blake's salty cock on my tongue and their voices filling my head, not to mention the visual stimulation of them being so close and hot for each other, my senses are seriously close to overload.

Blake lets out a sharp groan and jerks back. I follow the movement like a pro, keeping him secure in my mouth. I suck hard and deep, and within seconds, I'm rewarded with a strong burst of semen hitting the back of my throat. I swallow instinctively and a warm glow surrounds me as his essence slides down my throat. He tastes like forever.

Mine.

This time when Blake pulls back, I let his cock slip free, and then, before I can even think about moving on my own accord, he lifts me up and then they're surrounding me. Josh's mouth is hot and demanding on the back of my neck and shoulders while Blake's teeth torture me with small, searing bites along my jaw and throat. Hands grip my hips, kneading my flesh and making me writhe in between them, my senses exploding from the fierce onslaught.

Josh grabs my hair and pulls my head back to capture my mouth with his. As Blake's flavor floats between us, he moans.

"Delectable."

"Please," I hear myself whine. "I need you."

"Hush, kitten. Let us love you."

Blake's soft command weakens me, and I blink against a sudden welling of tears. I love them both so much, and to hear him say as much to me...it's more than I could have ever asked for.

"You're everything we've ever wanted, doll," Josh says soothingly from behind. "We want to make you ours."

I moan my agreement. "God, yes."

And then Blake lifts me again and cradles me against his hard chest. I wrap my arms around his neck and look over his shoulder to where Josh now stands waiting. His gaze is darker than I've ever seen it, and when Blake starts moving down the hall, Josh stalks behind us. I shiver at the unmistakable intent radiating from him.

The next thing I know, we're on Blake's king-sized bed and I'm being maneuvered into a half-sitting position in between Blake's legs, my back snug up against his abdomen. I gasp as he grabs my legs and stretches them wide, revealing my weeping pussy to Josh's hungry gaze.

I squirm against Blake's hold, desperate to feel his skin against my pussy, but before I can make any kind of progress, the sharp stab of his teeth sinking into the crook of my neck stills me.

"Do you know how gorgeous you are, spread out for me like some divine buffet?"

Josh holds my gaze and strips down to nothing. His cock bobs against his stomach as he crawls between my legs.

"Later, I'm going to lick your pussy until you scream, but right now, I need to be inside you, doll."

I nod, unable to speak past the lump in my throat. It's what I want too. More than anything.

Blake moves his legs to hook mine, making it impossible for me to move any more than a quarter of an inch, and then rolls my nipples between his fingers. Frissons of salacious need fly over my already sensitive nerve endings. I'm helpless between them. I have no choice but to accept whatever they decide to do.

I fucking love it.

Josh braces himself above me, and my breath hitches when he stops to give Blake a hot, tongue-filled kiss before lowering himself to me. His cock nudges my entrance, and if I could, I'd thrust my hips up to capture him with my heat, but I can't, so I whimper, hoping he'll take pity on me.

"Ah, you're so goddamn perfect, you know that?" Josh whispers. "Do you know how long we've waited for you, doll? For the one woman who could accept us this way?"

"Too long, kitten," Blake murmurs in my ear, not giving me a chance to respond. "From the second we saw you, we wanted you like this. Ours."

"Ours," Josh agrees.

And then Josh surges in, burying himself in my pussy with a harsh groan. A small cry escapes my lips from the sudden invasion.

"He's so hard for you, kitten."

I groan. I've been with Josh before, but this time, he feels massive inside me. He pulls out slowly and then thrusts back in fast, deep and hard. Within a few strokes, he's hit a flawless rhythm of mind-bending pleasure. He plays my G-spot with experienced precision, taking me higher with each plunge until my head is thrashing against Blake's chest with the need to let go.

"Give it to her," Blake rasps. "She's ready."

Josh ups the tempo just as Blake's hand finds my clit. He rubs hard circles on the hard nub, and I light up like a set of fireworks. Shots of exquisite pleasure pump through me like rapid gunfire. Blake holds me tight, not allowing my body to buck and heave like it wants to, giving Josh free access to fuck me hard and fast. It prolongs my orgasm, and I let loose a tortured scream as a second explosion rips through me. At that exact second, Josh jolts, and I feel his cock jerk inside of me, his cum filling me with jets of liquid heat.

The realization that we didn't use a condom hits me then, but I don't care. I'm on birth control and we're all clean. Besides, I couldn't imagine that impersonal latex intruding on the perfection of this moment.

"Mine," I whisper, my voice hoarse.

Josh leans in and kisses my lips. He's so gentle and loving, so giving. I reach up and pull Blake down for a kiss too, something inside me needing the confirmation of what we just did.

"Yours," they both answer, their voices layering each other and wrapping me up in their love.

I don't know if this means that all my dreams have come true, but at this moment, I have everything I've ever wanted, ever dreamed of, and that's all I can manage to determine before I surrender every part of myself to our euphoric union.

A THIEF IN
THE NIGHT

Giselle Renarde

The lock clicked and Derek sat straight up in bed.

In *Hailey's* bed.

What was that noise? There—that noise. The metallic *click, turn, squeak*. The squeal of rusty hinges. He must be dreaming or else living out a horror movie. His heart raced so wildly his breath couldn't keep up. What was happening here?

"Hailey." He found her arm and shook it. "Hailey, wake up. What was that noise?"

"Huh?" She rolled groggily away from him, mumbling words he didn't understand.

When the floorboards creaked, Derek's legs went numb. He whispered, "Hailey. Hailey? Someone's out there. Someone's *here.*"

Hailey bolted upright beside him, her hair a cloud of kinky curls. "Shit! I forgot…"

Creak, creak, creak.

"Forgot?" Derek became a frightened chipmunk. He couldn't

help it. "Forgot what? Forgot to lock the door?"

"No, not that." She settled into bed and threw off the covers, just enough to reveal her skimpy, silky nightie. "I forgot it was Thursday night. I should have canceled, but it's too late now."

"Canceled what, Hailey? What is this?"

They'd been out of each other's lives for years, but when they met in that supermarket two weeks ago it was like picking up exactly where they had left off. The friendship they had abandoned in eighth grade when they'd gone off to different high schools, was still there between them. Right away, he felt close to her again. Good ol' Hailey, the gorgeous girl next door. With every date, he felt like he knew her even better, inside and out.

Now Derek didn't know what to think. Somebody was sneaking around her apartment, and she seemed totally blasé about it. Seemed prepared for it, actually.

"Hailey, what's happening?"

"Shhh!" She closed her eyes, feigning sleep for some unknown reason. "Just go with it, okay? You'll enjoy it."

Before he could even think of how to respond, the bedroom door burst open. Through the blackness of the threshold, he could just make out a shape. A body: a man, all in black. Even his face was covered with a dark balaclava. All Derek could really see in the filtered moonlight was the gleam in his eyes.

"Hailey!" Derek tried to reach for her, but his body turned to stone. He couldn't even move his head. He could barely speak. "The phone. Where's the phone? Call the police."

"Looks like we've got company." The burglar chuckled deeply. His voice was dark as the devil, the black rumble of a thundering bass line. "I wasn't expecting a man in bed, but I guess I can play along."

"Play?" Derek's heart jumped into his throat as the burglar approached the bed. He was still trying to make sense of Hailey's instructions to "just go with it." "Look, we don't want any trouble. My wallet's in my back pocket. Pants are on the floor, right there—oh, you're stepping on them. Don't step on them!"

"So sorry," the burglar said, his voice dripping with sarcasm. "Would you like me to pick them up? Fold them for you? How about I take them to get dry-cleaned? My treat."

Derek watched as the thief tore the leather belt from his stepped-on pants. "What's that for?"

The man in black pursed his lips. "I think we both know what it's for."

Without another word, the stranger set a huge gloved hand on Derek's shoulder and heaved him forward. Derek told his limbs to flail. He told himself to fight, but nothing happened. He seemed to have gone completely numb, neither able to fight or flee. The man yanked his hands behind his back and wrapped his belt around his wrists again and again, tightening the leather until he could slip its black tongue through the silver buckle.

After the big burglar secured that belt around Derek's wrists, he left him kneeling on the mattress. "I'm guessing you like to watch."

"Why would you think that?" Derek asked, even though he was really thinking, *How could you possibly know?*

Hailey.

She hadn't moved a muscle. All the commotion, and she lay there like a sleeping angel, pretending to be as helpless as she appeared. She knew this guy. This must be some kind of game they played: guy breaks into girl's apartment, takes her in her sleep. Did people really do stuff like that? Apparently.

"Now, what have we here?" The stranger walked around to the other side of Hailey's big bed. Kneeling on the floor, he traced one gloved finger down her cheek, all the way to her chin. She didn't react. Didn't even crack a smile.

The man in black tilted his cocky head up and looked Derek straight in the eye. "Is she your girlfriend, mate?"

"What the hell do you think you're doing?"

"She's a tasty morsel, eh?" The big guy pushed the covers aside and pulled up Hailey's nightie. "Oooh, a shaved pussy! Did she do that for you, then?"

Derek struggled against his bindings, but his limbs were like anchors. "Get your hands off my girlfriend!"

"Oh, so she *is* your girlfriend." The stranger opened Hailey's sweet, soft pussy lips with two gloved fingers. Staring at the glistening pink wetness of her folds, he said, "You must be incensed just now, watching a thief in the night touch your pretty girlfriend's cunt."

"Yes," Derek said, in barely a whisper. Why was he salivating as the stranger plunged one thick finger between those naked lips?

"Mmm..." Hailey shifted just slightly, but her eyes didn't open.

"Your girlfriend likes that, doesn't she?" The burglar fucked her slowly, making her pussy sing with sloppy squelching sounds. "Oooh, she likes how I fuck her. Hear how she's purring, pal? Just like a kitty."

"Yeah." Derek watched the taut black leather of that man's glove disappear into Hailey's cunt, then reappear smeared with her juices. His jaw swung open. He sat and stared, mesmerized by the motion.

"Bet you're jealous," the burglar said. "Bet you're just itching to get at this sweet little pussy."

"Yeah," Derek repeated, and swallowed hard.

"Bet you're craving the taste." The big guy slowly withdrew his thick finger from the "sleeping" Hailey's pussy. He stuck out his tongue like he was going to lick it, and when Derek lurched forward, he laughed. "You're jealous, all right. You love eating her pussy, don't you?"

Derek was drooling, panting, beastly in his need. "Yeah, I do. I love it. God, I love it so much."

"You been eating her pussy long?" the burglar asked, in a way that made Derek think he must be raising an eyebrow under that black ski mask.

"No, not long. I mean, we've known each other forever. Like, literally forever. We went to school together, until we were fourteen or so. We only met back up again two weeks ago," he babbled.

"Ahh." The man in black nodded knowingly. "I bet you love her, don't you?"

"Love?" Derek felt suddenly flustered. "I haven't...I mean, sure I do, but we...oh god..."

A flash of pain crossed Derek's temples, throbbing where his skull met his brain. This was too much. Christ, now he was getting dizzy and worried he might faint. He wished Hailey would say something.

The thief grabbed his shoulder with one hand and passed the other under his nose, like smelling salts. "Hey, it's okay, mate. Stay with me. We're good, here."

Derek barely felt conscious as he extended his tongue toward the burglar's leather-clad finger. He followed the musky scent until his tongue found the dense, aromatic source. *Pussy.* He'd know that taste anywhere. And Hailey's pussy was so special, so unique, that Derek found himself sucking the burglar's finger, savoring that thick digit like a woman-flavored candy cane.

When it occurred to him that he actually had his mouth wrapped around a strange man's finger, Derek got that stabbing feeling like someone was jamming an ice pick into his eye. This was stress on top of stress, and yet he was strangely calmed by the very thing that generated it.

Pulling away from the thief's finger, he said, "Fuck her. More."

The thief spread Hailey's pussy lips with two fingers. As he thrust slowly inside her, Hailey gurgled gently. She rolled her body just enough for her nightie strap to tumble down one shoulder, revealing her beautiful brown breast. It looked so soft, so sweet with sleep that Derek wanted to launch his face at it. But he could barely move, even now. The burglar called all the shots.

"You should..." Derek swallowed hard, looking for courage. "You should suck her nipple. I think she'd like that."

"You think?"

"Yeah." Derek struggled to sound reasonable and rational in this bizarre situation. "It's closer to you, anyway."

The thief chuckled, slow and dark as molasses. Pulling his fingers from between Hailey's thighs, he hooked his thumb around the nightie strap near Derek and pulled it down. Derek's mouth filled with saliva as he watched Hailey's delicious breast peek out from under a fine layer of silk. Her face was soft and relaxed, and her skin had that smell he loved, of a warm, aroused woman. He didn't know what the hell was happening, and he didn't care anymore. All he wanted in the world was to wrap his lips around Hailey's sweet nipple and suck it until she made some noise.

"Go on," said the thief in the night. "You suck that one. I've got the other."

Derek gazed suspiciously at the stranger. "You're not going to head-butt me when I bend forward, are you?"

The guy laughed raucously, and still Hailey didn't open her eyes.

"Was that a no?"

"No, I'm not going to head-butt you."

"Okay, then..." Derek let his head drop and his body fall forward. He felt like a felled tree tumbling to the forest floor. *Timberrr!*

When his mouth met Hailey's soft skin, he felt a subtle jump inside her. She faked it well, but he knew she couldn't be sleeping through an encounter like this. No one could. Hailey was playing possum, pretending not to know what was going on. But what sort of kinky game was it she was playing?

Derek glanced up as the man in the balaclava inserted three firm fingers into his girlfriend's cunt. "Who are you?"

A spark ignited in the burglar's eyes. He laughed. "Just a thief in the night, mate."

Sinking against Hailey's chest, the thief licked her dark nipple, summoning it to erection. That wasn't the only thing that got unmistakably hard as Derek watched the stranger's big pink tongue lapping his girlfriend's tit. His mind swirled like a cyclone. His cock throbbed. If he eased his hips back and forth just gently, he could eke out mild stimulation from his belly and his thighs. It wasn't nearly enough, but it was something.

Hailey's pussy squelched rudely with every pass from the stranger's thick gloved fingers. He curved his thumb around her clit, working so hard Derek sensed the response in his girlfriend's muscles. Her belly rippled like a pond. Her thighs tensed and released. Even in the moonlight, he could see her response. But more than that, he could feel the orgasm rising in her body.

Together, the stranger and Derek worshipped Hailey's breasts. When the man in black stopped licking and started sucking, Derek followed suit, like he was taking unspoken instruction from the guy who'd broken into his girlfriend's apartment.

With their heads resting one against the other, they suckled lovely Hailey, making her writhe and moan. Finally, some response! Derek had been waiting for this since the burglar first broke in. He wanted Hailey to react. He wanted her to *do* something.

And she did: she grabbed Derek's hair with one hand and the burglar's balaclava with the other, holding both men in place as they caressed her breasts. Just the feel of Hailey's hand on his head sent Derek's imagination swirling out of control. In a single moment, he experienced their entire life together, from the innocent crush he'd had on her when they were young, through the moment he'd spotted her at the supermarket and thought his heart would give out, right up to this very moment, tied up by an intruder, sucking her breasts in the wee hours of the morning.

His cock swelled against his thighs as he shifted and bucked. When he pressed his heels closer together, they found his balls and squeezed those sensitive orbs. He was unbelievably close to coming as he savored Hailey's nipple and shared in her joy of being possessed by a mysterious stranger.

"Yes," Hailey murmured. "Please...more!"

Derek couldn't see her face from this angle, but he'd bet any money her eyes were still closed. Her body twisted against the mattress. From the sounds of her cries, she was biting her bottom lip, stifling the chaos of her orgasm.

She was trying to keep quiet, trying not to react. That's what sent Derek over the edge—not her intensity, but her attempt to conceal it. He had no idea why that turned him on so much, but he couldn't argue with his dick. It shot warm ropes of come across his chest as he slid his tongue in wide circles around Hailey's nipple. They climaxed together, while a stranger in black fucked her with his fat gloved fingers.

What happened after that? His head started spinning. The room grew darker than before. He tried to stay conscious, but the haze of shock and bliss took over. Hailey's soft panting filled his dizzy mind while the stranger extracted his fingers from her pussy.

"Shall I leave him like that?" the burglar asked. "You'll undo the belt?"

"Yes, I'll get it," Hailey whispered. "Thanks for not freaking out. I didn't plan this, you know. It just happened."

The man in black chuckled, but if he said anything more, Derek didn't catch it. He didn't totally come back into reality until he felt Hailey unbuckling his belt and freeing his hands. Until that moment, he hadn't realized how tense his muscles had become. They twinged when he moved them, and painful pins and needles set in.

"Oh boy." Rolling onto his back, he tried to shake out his hands, but they fell uselessly at his sides. His legs had frozen up, too. Breaking out of his folded-over position only generated more pain. "Wow, that hurts."

"Sorry."

"It's not your fault."

Hailey kissed his forehead. "Yes, it is."

"Hailey?"

"Hmm?"

Derek tried to clench his fists, but his fingers wouldn't respond. "That guy..."

She sighed. "Sorry about that."

"It's okay." Derek tried to curl his toes, but an impotent tremble coursed through his legs. Released from his bindings, he still couldn't move. "Who was he?"

"Don't worry." Hailey rubbed his tingling arm. "I'll tell him not to come again."

"No," Derek said, betraying himself with a smile. "He can come as often as he likes."

DRINKING GAMES WITH COWBOYS

Axa Lee

I hadn't seen Keith in nearly three years, not since college. So when he Facebooked me to say he was passing my way on his way north, I took him up on the offer to stop by. Justin and I had been fighting again, our on-again-off-again relationship definitely on the off. I needed a night out with the guys.

I was seventeen when I learned to love the skill of older men; men aged at least forty. Twenty years older than me works ideally. But in this society, it's almost taboo to date even a decade above my own age bracket, which is currently a quarter century, so discretion is a must. So poor Justin (twenty-eight, I might add, a far cry from the "no dick under thirty" rule I held to at twenty) is stuck not only worrying about the good-looking guys I farm with and the occasional savvy farm girl I meet, but guys over forty as well. Well, he *was* stuck. He can now stick it. What can I say? A mature man is my weakness. If they're cowboys, I swoon.

Guilford is with Keith when they pull in to pick me up. I

throw my arms around Keith, barely able to reach around his shoulders, he's so tall and I'm what he calls "vertically challenged." I shove Guil in the shoulder when he teases me that I should carry a box to stand on for situations like this. He's a bull rider, sometime bullfighter, an indifferent roper and only a few inches taller than me. I call Guil a pussy for missing the Reed City rodeo the previous weekend. A lot of people think there isn't any decent rodeo in Michigan, and no cowboys. They are so wrong.

"They ain't got no bulls," he says. I scoff. They do have bulls, good ones, and he knows it.

"Chasin' work or chasin' tail?" I say.

"Ain't that the same thing?" Keith says.

Guil's a farrier and most of his clients are women. He's famous for his "full-service" horse trimming and shoeing business.

I jump in the truck between them, grab an MGD off the floorboards of Keith's old beater truck. The truck coughs as Keith shifts it into gear.

Beer never tastes as good as it does with Keith and Guil.

I'm grinning, sitting there between my boys, as we booze cruise through the cool spring night, bodies packed tightly on the bench seat. We turn the radio up, singing badly to Willie and Waylon and the boys. It thrills me, being pressed next to Keith. I've missed him so much. I've missed *this*. Getting off the farm on a warm night, cold beer, good friends and a back road. Justin's had me so wrapped up in his drama (he wants me to get back together, move in with him, get a "big girl job" and sell the horses; I, in short, don't) that my head aches. Getting back to this—banter between men over which one humps sheep, which one is gayer than the other, which one would be more likely to bring a fat girl home from the bar, the bragging and bravado— is what I've needed.

"So that ol' bitch whips back"—Keith's in the middle of a story—"and lambasts numb-nuts here right in the face. Never saw it comin'."

"I beg to differ." Guil goes all formal, which just makes me laugh harder. "I saw her comin', what I lacked was the opportunity to duck since some asshole didn't have the wherewithal to give a dude a heads-up."

"Bitches be crazy," I say.

"Especially Angus bitches," Keith adds.

"You keep your damn shit-horn poly-red snides," Guil says. He and Keith have never agreed on cattle. It's a lot like the Pepsi versus Coke debate; neither camp will ever convince the other different.

My stomach clenches at being so close to Keith after all this time. I can't even tell you how many nights I've used the memory of his Robert Duvall demeanor, Monty Python sense of humor and Tom Selleck good looks to get off with another guy, usually a younger and less-experienced guy. And by less experienced I mean fumbling, by younger I mean thirty and by guy I mean I'm usually tougher than he is. But that's not the case now, not with these two.

"It's not like I don't love him," I tell the boys over beer and burgers at the local dive bar. It's the kind of backwoods place you can go to after working cows, when your clothes are covered in blood, snot and shit and no one bats an eye. Especially if its karaoke night. "I do. Madly. It's just…"

I sigh and stack my fries into a fort in the red basket, lined with greasy paper. Justin's a great guy, don't get me wrong. But I've come to think he's great for someone else. Another over-qualified engineer with a self-inflated ego, perhaps. I've never cheated on him. Technically we're on a break, but a break with booty calls. My biggest fear is that we'll get married, have lots of babies, get cellulite together, and one day I'll have had enough and while clearing the dinner table one night will brain him with a pork chop bone. The writing was on the wall. No, the writing had made the wall its bitch. I could sum up all of Justin's problems in four words: he wasn't a cowboy.

"He comes from a certain background and it's not broncs and bulls. He's never been poor. He's never had to work for anything. He's never been hurt. He has certain expectations and I don't...I'm not it. I don't think I'm the partner he's looking for. He thinks I am," I add, looking up into Keith's startlingly blue gaze. I've always loved his eyes. I take in how the past few years have grayed his black hair and how his last rodeo injury, broken ribs from a runaway bronc that threw him into some gates, makes him those few seconds slower. Someone else might not notice, that he grimaces holding the door for me, or pauses, sucking in a sharp breath, before lowering himself all the way onto a chair. I do. It's still him though, and I couldn't be gladder that he's here, with me.

Keith smiles under his black mustache. It's still black and neatly trimmed, extending down either side of his chin.

"We could go to Texas," he jokes. "Spend the winter training horses."

I laugh. He's said this before, when I used to sneak into his trailer at night. Ranch hands where we worked weren't supposed to sleep together. So for almost two years we calved cows and broke horses, and sometimes equipment, together during the day and made the other cry out in pleasure at night. He'd had a radio on in the trailer and Jo Dee Messina was singing "Heads Carolina, Tails California."

"Hmm..." I'd said, nuzzling into the heat of his arm as we lay naked in the cool light of a waning moon. "I don't like scorpions or snakes."

"Oklahoma?" he said into my hair. "Kentucky?"
I'd been so in love with this man.

"Sure glad I'm still awesome, unlike you two sad sacks."
Guil laughs, shakes his head.

John Adam Guilford is his real name, but no one calls him
that. He's of an age with Keith, but will assure you that he's
younger by a whopping seven months. John's Mexican-dark,
where Keith's just dark haired with a fair complexion. They're
both fathers and grandfathers, divorced cowboys who text and
use Facebook and rodeo with the best of 'em.

The conversation turns to horses and cattle and dogs, as it
always does with us. Keith and I are too much alike: Scorpios,
Western film and book addicts, Quarter Horse lovers, Arabian
haters, blue heeler owners, sheep despisers and Wrangler
wearers. Keith's a big man, six-foot-two, two hundred pounds
give or take, depending on how much fast food he eats, broad
shoulders, built like an old-time cowboy. He's a ringer for Tom
Sellek in the movie *Monte Walsh,* from battered gray hat to
broken-down boots and I love everything in between.

Guil's nature lightens the emotional atomic bombs that are
Keith and me. His is the black cowboy hat to Keith's battered
gray. Both of these men at one time showed me my worth when
I didn't believe in it myself. It's the gift of older men. That and
trying to turn me into a sorry roper from an abysmal one.

It starts with dancing at the bar. Keith's not a dancer and,
I suspect, is too beat up anyway. He said he'd been "ropin'
steers for an ol' boy up t' home," throwing down five hundred
pounders to vaccinate with nothing but a crippled old farmer in
a blue mechanic's jumpsuit and a heeler dog for help. Guil, on
the other hand, is Rico Suave. He twirls me around the floor,
dancing as easily to Johnny Cash as he does to Jay-Z. He's the
more outgoing of the two, absolutely comfortable with himself,

and knows all the rap songs, since he only chases women under thirty since his divorce. He has to be cool in order to get laid.

I talk the boys out of trying to rope deer out of the back of Keith's pickup, since it worked out so badly the last time. And back at my place I turn music on and Guil dances up on me in the kitchen while I slice limes for some tequila. I swat him away and he pulls beers out of the fridge for the three of us while Keith shuffles cards for a game. Finally I prove such a poor euchre player that out of sympathy (or frustration at three-handed drunk euchre) they switch to waterfall.

"What are the rules again?" Keith asks.

"Don't worry," Guil says, "you'll pick it up as we go along."

The rules, I find, typically tend to wander as the drinking progresses.

Play begins pretty typically. Draw a six, chicks drink. Draw a five, guys drink. Draw a king, everyone drinks. Draw an ace and it's waterfall, where the player who drew the card begins to drink, then the next, and the next, until it's back to the player who drew the card and he can stop, followed by the next player and the next. It works better with a bunch of people.

I'm on Keith's lap and he's palming my tits, while Guil and I argue over whether the ten card is for Chinese Fire Drill or take off one article of clothing.

"Call it, K," Guil says. Keith pretends to ignore him as he rolls my breasts in his huge hands, then looks up, feigning confusion.

"Oh," he says. "Present." And smiles.

Guil throws up his hands, and drinks anyway.

The game really begins to dissolve when we all three have to take off our shirts (jack = new rule) and especially when Guil takes a shot of tequila off my boobs (8 = mate, choose someone to drink with, which Guil interpreted as choose someone to drink off of). I'm not a well-endowed girl, but pushup bras work wonders.

It's the lick that does it. There's a linger. You know that linger. Every woman knows that linger. Where someone you never noticed before, sexually, notices you, and you notice back.

Guil licks the salt off my chest, then dives for the lime. But when he goes for the shot, he lingers. He watches me and I watch him.

"Goddamn, girl," he says, "you are really good lookin'."

I scoff. "You're drunk."

"No, really, I'd marry you. Beluga, wouldn't I marry her?"

Beluga was Keith's nickname, something to do with his size being thought to be equivalent to that of a baby beluga whale at one time or another. Or his penis being thought to be the size of...well, you get the idea.

"You'd marry anything with legs, Guilford." Keith's voice is thick-drunk. We're all pretty toasty.

"New rule!" Guil declares, even though he hasn't drawn a card, let alone a jack. "Audrey's mouth on my cock."

"I don't think so!" I laugh.

"You're always sayin' how much you like head, girl, prove it." Guil's unbuckling his belt.

I look at Keith, the silent question passing between us. I'm already down to bra and panties, thanks to Guil's "no shirt, no shoes" rule. Why that involved no pants as well is one of those indecipherable questions for the gods of alcohol, but Keith and I had gone along with it.

"Oh, what the hell," I say, "Whip out the grasshopper."

Guil covers himself as if I've hurt his penis's feelings.

"Ouch!" he says. "You'll scare the lil' guy."

I'm laughing as I take his cock in my mouth, running my teeth down the shaft just to give Guil a hard time. He sucks air through his teeth, but takes my wordless ribbing without complaint. I'm just fucking with him really, using my teeth (gently), excessive saliva, overusing my hand, excessive pornographic moans, all the things guys complain about when they get bad blow jobs.

"Oh my god, baby," I say in my best faux–porn star, "it's too big!"

We're positioned so Keith can watch; I pull back, rolling my eyes and scoffing. But the look in Keith's eyes, that heavy, dark expression, makes me pause. I touch my tongue to the head of Guil's cock and Keith shifts in his chair. He's enjoying this, I realize, watching me. I do it again, roll my tongue around Guil's cock and hear a barely perceptible noise come from Keith. I smile at him.

"You make me feel like a twenty-year-old kid again," Keith told me once. And for a moment I wish he was. He's the only guy I've ever met whose kids I'd have in a moment, though his kids are my age, or a little older, and he's already a grandfather.

"Goddamn, girl." Guil sucks in his breath.

Keith rises, apparently tired of watching. He lies on the floor behind me. It takes some maneuvering, but in the end, I'm blowing Guil while Keith eats my pussy. His tongue dives into my pussy again and again. I'm so hard. My clit feels like an aching knob, craving the tip of tongue and nipping of teeth. He doesn't disappoint. I've never found a guy who can eat pussy and loves it as much as Keith. For most guys, it's a chore, a necessary evil to get their own rocks off, but I think Keith would be happy to stay there for hours and never get bored or resentful. And neither would I. His ex-wife's loss.

Keith explores every inch—the lips, the clit, from front to back—letting me stay on top, since it's more comfortable for him. His hips don't lock up with me above him. He sucks, licks and teases me until I have to pull away from Guil as I buck and gasp, shuddering above Keith like a paint-bucket shaker at the hardware store, until he has to reach up and still me, his fingers almost meeting to circle the circumference of my hips. Guil palms my breasts as I come.

I want to cry with how much I've missed Keith. He was the last guy I came with before Justin. He runs his big hand down the curve of my breast to my hip and swears softly. I'm not a girl of nineteen anymore and though I'm still five foot nothin', I've lost weight since he last saw me, am lean and fit and have come into my own. He's still scarred, with one twisted leg and the danger of locking up one day like the Tin Man from Oz and never regaining mobility. He's still fit and strong, but with the beginnings of a paunch that I don't mind.

Guil's cock bobs in front of my face. I wrap my hand around his shaft and stroke up and down it with a loose fist. He's slick with precum so my hand slides easily.

Keith takes little nips and licks once in a while, but mostly he watches what's going on above him. He always loved watching me with a dick.

You can tell a lot about a guy from his cock. If it's too small, he's a Napoleon, steer clear. If it's too big, he's a player and you'll join the legions of girls who can't deep-throat him and the ones who can are just nasty. Besides, a huge dick will knock the bottom out of your cervix and you'll hate me for it because I warned you, so avoid. Most guys fall in the in-between, too small and holy-shit-on-a-whole-wheat-cracker-mother-of-god-what-is-that-thing? I'd expected more from Guil. With all the stories about his sexual exploits and lonely 4-H horse-show moms, you'd think he'd have "seven inches of solid meat" to work with (his tasteful description, not mine), where instead he boasted something more reasonable, smaller, but firm, something I could deep-throat with ease.

I hold his hips and roll my tongue around his cock. I tease the head, then take all of it in my mouth, doing mini-pulses at the bottom. Guil's fingers tighten in my hair.

"Oh yeah," he groans. "You're going to get me off you keep doin' that."

"That's the idea," I say.

He's so hard right now and my saliva is drying up fast from all the alcohol. I add my hand to his shaft and hurry the pace a little, trying to get him to come before my mouth goes completely dry.

I shouldn't worry though. Precum slips out suddenly and coats the length of his dick. His head drops back, fingers rest just behind my ears, gently guiding the pace he likes, lightly ramming into my face again and again. Now Keith's finger is on my clit, stroking me, urging me, and I think I hear his hand on his cock behind me, feel his arm move in a steady rhythm. I rock forward and back on Guil's cock, as Keith's fingers rub over and over my cunt. I'm fighting not to choke. I'm fighting to breathe. *Steady, through the nose,* I tell myself. I'm fighting not to come, but when Keith hits just the right spot, when Guil stiffens, pumping shallowly, gasping, I lose, and clench hard over Keith, as Guil's fingers tighten on my scalp and I have to swallow quickly, swallowing his bitter cum down, stroking him, releasing him, quivering as I collapse in the circle of Keith's arm.

In that moment, I love Guil too, a little. I love every guy I fuck a little. You have to. But loving them doesn't mean you stay together forever. Was I lingering and agonizing over Justin because I really loved him or because I loved the orgasms? Why do I think too hard after I come?

Guil's knees don't want to hold him, and he sinks down on a chair.

"So was I right?" I say to Guil. "Told you I give an amazing blow job."

"Yeah, you can blow me any day," he pants, and I laugh.

Keith's shoulder is warm beneath my cheek. I missed his heat, his touch, his laugh, his smile. I missed working together and coming out after a snowstorm to find he'd started my car and turned the AC on. Twisted bastard and his sense of humor. It matches my own.

My hand is level with Keith's waist. He guides it to his cock. I stroke him and press my head into the softness of his shoulder.

Keith guides me down to ride his cock, which I do with great enthusiasm. I don't bend my head for him to kiss me. That, I feel, is asking a bit much. He feels so good inside me. At first, I just sink down on the length of him, letting him fill me, then I begin to ride him, sliding up until I feel his cockhead just at the edge of my opening and press back down. My head falls back as I shiver in pleasure. He undulates his hips against me. This is a horseman after all. I roll my hips against his, picking up the pace, groaning and squeezing. He does a half sit-up, moaning, arching into me.

He entwines his fingers with mine and his bracing grip gives me the balance to ride him until both of us are jerking and shaking. White lights burst behind my eyes as my pussy pulses on its own again and again. He bucks when he comes, blowing out his nose like a bull or stud horse, tossing his head side to side, his big hands circling my hips and hauling me close. He gives himself over to the orgasm completely and his bad leg jerks as we collapse in sweat and cum.

It takes me a while to come back to myself, to not feel the weird disembodiment between past and present. I want this. I've wanted this for three years. I've missed Keith so much, his sense of humor and competency with a horse. And I won't lose that, won't lose people who understand what it means to love the land more than you love anyone else. Justin has never understood that, and he never will, I realize. He'll always want me to be different, to be better, when all I need to be happy is cold beer and good friends. I can't, I won't, go back to Justin after this. Life is too short to worry about someone who's always harping at you, worrying over what you "should" do.

We're hung over as shit the next morning, but we're each smiling. Keith kisses me good-bye and my heart constricts. There's no future here; I know that. I understand. His life is waning, his prime is over, mine's just beginning. But I don't really care. I'd still run off with him to anywhere and have his babies if he seriously asked me to. I'm sick of being, as Guil put it, a sad sack over Justin. It might be the wrong choice. I might regret this. *Might*. But I *know* I'll regret it if I pass up this chance and go back to Justin. Young men are just...young. There's no depth, no experience, no interesting conversation, just uncontrollable horniness and an obsession with quoting Will Ferrell movies. For right now, this is what I need. Good friends, good beer, good times. The rest will come when I'm ready. I'm not thirty; I have no ties. I still have time to be awesome with my friends.

"See you at the rodeo next weekend." Guil flicks my hat, almost but not quite knocking it off my head before I catch it. "I'll be the one who actually *catches* his steer."

"Gonna show up this time, chickenshit?" I razz him.

"He'll be the one roping with the pink rope, with the little girls," Keith says.

"Beluga, I don't wanna hear it outta you," Guil blusters.

"Yeah? Whaddya gonna do? Throw your pink cowboy boots at me?"

"Nah, his man-gina's acting up. Just like it will next weekend and he'll have all kinda excuses then too," I tease.

Guil leans out the truck window and tries to flick my hat again, but I dodge, smiling. He looks over at Keith. "You gonna drive that truck or sit there strokin' the gearshift all day?"

"I'm drivin'," Keith says, "you worry about coverin' your bull. I got ya."

"See you next weekend," I say to them.

"I'll buy ya a beer when you miss," Guil says.

"Oh, it is *so* on," I say.

It so was.

THE LAST DAY OF SUMMER

Veronica Wilde

It was almost fall, but the August sun was still strong as I stepped outside to tan for the last time that summer. I placed a chilled bottle of water, my headphones and iPod, and a bottle of coconut-scented tanning oil next to my poolside lounge. The pool was a serene aqua, waiting for that moment when I couldn't stand the sun any longer and needed to dive into cool water. Pulling my blonde hair into a ponytail, I stared at its surface and wondered who I would be skinny-dipping with later tonight. Mia, my summer playmate? Or Kevin, the crush I had managed to seduce this summer?

Mia's long black hair and perfect breasts rose up in my mind—and so did Kevin's mop of brown hair and sexy ice-blue eyes. As always, I sighed with yearning at the thought of them. I dropped my towel on the other side of the lounge chair, then glanced around my mother's backyard. Cornfields stood on one side, a fence on the other. Out here in the country, there was no one to see me—so I pulled off my black bikini and luxuriated

naked in the sunshine. Time to begin my last day of freedom.
And decide who to spend it with.

I had been unemployed for five months. That had meant
moving back in with my mother in my small rural hometown
where nothing ever happened. But I'd finally found a job right
here close to home and I started tomorrow—so I was headed
back to the nine-to-five world of cubicles and business clothes.
I looked forward to having a paycheck and my own apartment
again, even if my mother wouldn't have minded me continuing
to live with her, and I really wanted to spend my last day of
freedom in sexual heaven.

My mother was off at some church retreat, which made
it even more of a holiday for me. As if it wasn't bad enough
moving back in with my mom at twenty-six, it was made even
worse by the fact that she refused to let me have any dates sleep
over for the night. But now she was gone until tomorrow, and
that meant I could indulge myself in style. As I settled naked
into my lounge chair, I tried to decide who I should invite over:
Mia or Kevin? Normally my dates with both of them were
brief, hot trysts that they fit in before or after work. Mia lived
with her parents too, and Kevin had roommates, so we rarely
had any sustained privacy. This was my chance to have a long
extravagant bondage scene with Mia, until we fell asleep next
to each other in my childhood bed and cuddled all night long.
Or maybe I could have a romantic night with Kevin, having sex
outside in the moonlight as the crickets serenaded us. Which
one should it be?

Kevin had been my high school dream. He was a senior
when I was a freshman, a tall, coolly gorgeous basketball
player oblivious to my existence. I had pined desperately for
his pale-blue bedroom eyes and languid smile, but of course he
never noticed me. I couldn't believe my luck when I moved back

here and discovered he was still in town, newly divorced and sexy as ever. After he bought me a drink at the local bar one night, he made all my wishes come true. We had been seeing each other ever since. Unfortunately, I suspected he had other women all over town and so I'd tried not to get attached. He was my unemployment summer fling, I kept reminding myself. Nothing more.

A week after meeting Kevin, I walked into an ice-cream shop and spotted a hazel-eyed goddess. Though she'd been a few years behind me in school, I knew who she was—Mia Scott, the best softball player our town had ever produced. Apparently a rotator cuff injury had torpedoed her scholarship and she was back home for a while as well. Tanned and lithe, with long black hair falling down her back, she had the sultry eyes of a tigress. When our gazes locked, I knew she was the kind of girl who would be able to tie me up and tease me just the way I needed. We flirted outrageously and within two days, I had my second summer lover.

They didn't know about each other. But we'd never said we were exclusive—and they were both so sexy that I was sure they were dating other people too. I'd seen women throw themselves at Kevin right in front of me, after all. And Mia, well, she was so cool and remote that I never knew what she was thinking or feeling. So I tried to remind myself that we were all just having fun, no strings attached. That I wasn't really falling for either of them—even though I knew in my heart that I was falling for both of them.

The sun baked into my skin, golden and sensual. I'd been tanning all summer to look sexy for them, wrinkles be damned. My mind turned to thoughts of Mia tying my hands behind my back and slowly stroking my clit while I begged her to let me come. Bondage had always been my weakness, guaranteed to make me melt, and Mia knew exactly how to excite me. Kevin was more of a master cocksman, driving me crazy with his tongue and thick cock. With just one touch, he could make me wet and aching.

So once again I turned to the question of who I should spend my last day and night of freedom with. I turned my iPod to a sexy playlist, letting the sun lull me into a trance. I wanted to have a romantic last night before going back to work. This was my chance to say to Mia or Kevin, I'll be getting my own apartment and you can stay overnight all the time now. I just didn't know if those words would be welcome or not—if either of them secretly wanted me to be more than a summer fling. If so, who did I have a better chance with? Mia or Kevin?

The sun's warmth on my nipples felt so good that I opened my legs as well, letting my feet dangle on either side of the chair as the summer heat greeted my pussy. I drifted into a sensual drowsiness, dreaming of Mia's beautiful breasts and Kevin's hard thighs. My blood warmed with arousal. In fact, I could almost have sworn someone was there, touching me.

A metal clink brought me to full alertness. What the hell? I opened my eyes, suddenly aware I'd been napping. The pool waters danced merrily, no one in sight.

I tried to remove my headphones—and realized my wrists were locked to the chair. Shock turned to outrage as someone lifted off my headphones.

"Easy," Mia said. She walked around the length of the chair in shorts and a green tank top, never taking her eyes from my nakedness. "You're safe, Cheyenne. No need to freak out."

Well, that settled it. Mia it was. And what an afternoon we were about to have, a surprise poolside bondage scene just like I had always fantasized about.

I was about to say something saucy when a male voice said,

"Oh, come on. You know Cheyenne. She loves the feeling of danger."

Kevin joined her. They both regarded me like I was their captive.

Oh no. No.

"What did you do to me?" I squeaked. I didn't know if I was more disturbed by my powerlessness or the excitement rising in my blood.

"Something you've always wanted, apparently." Kevin stood between my spread legs and gazed at my exposed pussy.

Heat and arousal washed through me with almost painful intensity. I could tell now that they had locked my dangling ankles into a spreader bar, then cuffed my wrists beneath the chair. I was spread-eagle, naked and helpless. They could see every inch of me, could use my body any way they pleased. I thrashed against the lounge chair, as confused as I was turned on. How had they met?

"I have no idea what kind of game you two are playing—"

"Game we're playing? You're the one who's been two-timing us all summer." Mia stared at me coolly.

"Bullshit. We never agreed to be exclusive." I struggled at my restraints till I realized how much they enjoyed watching my breasts jiggle and bounce.

"We all know you're hoping one of us would do something like this. Or both of us," Kevin said. "Weren't you?"

"Yes," I whispered. This was my fantasy. The two of them.

He leaned over and stroked my pussy with one light finger, from the base of my slit up to my hardened clit. I moaned. He laughed and retreated. I tried to close my knees as much as I could.

Mia snapped her fingers. "Legs open," she ordered. "Show us your pussy. Show us how wet and swollen you are."

I obeyed.

"Good girl." Kevin sat on the edge of the chair and idly caressed my breasts.

My nipples were so hot and aching it was painful. If only Kevin would suck them, do something. I shifted in the chair, opening my legs wider in a hint.

"So," Kevin continued. He began tracing circles around my nipples until I wanted to scream. "You've been a busy girl this summer."

"Listen," I said weakly. I knew my behavior looked bad. Mia and Kevin knew about each other. And I was bound and naked. Which meant I was way too turned on to mount a skilled verbal defense on my own behalf. "I don't know how you two met—"

"You mean how we found out about each other. It's a small town, Cheyenne."

"Yeah, Cheyenne. Did you think we wouldn't find out?"

"Come on...you both have dated other people—"

"I haven't," Mia said. "Just you, all summer."

"Yeah, I haven't either," said Kevin.

They looked at each other. "Well, maybe we should start," Mia suggested.

"No," I blurted helplessly as they began to undress each other. Mia stared into his eyes as Kevin lifted up her top, exposing that flat, tanned stomach and the swell of her breasts in her lace bra cups. He stared at them with a dreamy grin. She smiled confidently and unhooked her bra, proudly revealing those perfect, firm tits. *Goddammit.* I swallowed, my mouth going dry. She was so gorgeous, she could have starred in any centerfold.

They leaned in and kissed each other, Kevin touching her nipples. I could barely breathe from the excitement and anguish. My two lovers were getting it on over my naked body and I was horrified they would prefer each other to me, and yet thrilled by the sight at the same time. I watched as Mia pushed down Kevin's pants, giggling as his hard cock sprang up to greet her. He slid down her shorts and rubbed her clit. I was getting wetter and hornier by the second and couldn't even touch myself. I wriggled in frustration.

"You are very sexy," Kevin told Mia. "Cheyenne's been a bad girl, keeping you to herself."

"Likewise," Mia replied, stroking his cock. "So what kind of things do you two do together?"

Kevin shrugged. "Nothing too wild," he said. "I mean, you know Cheyenne. She's kind of lazy in bed. Always wanting to be tied up and fucked."

"That's not fair!" I shouted from the lounge chair. "You like it too—"

"Same here," Mia told him. "The first time I tied her to the coffee table and ate her out, she came on the spot."

"Sounds like we've both spoiled her."

They regarded me with teasing disdain, then began to kiss each other again.

Oh god. There was nothing I could do but watch as they did all the things to each other that I'd done to them so many times—Kevin's tongue on Mia's dark-pink nipples, Mia tickling Kevin's balls. It was like watching the hottest porn ever, and even in my misery, I congratulated myself on landing two such sexy bedmates this summer.

But what was their plan? Were they really going to have sex with each other in front of me while I watched, leaving me unsatisfied? Or did I simply need to grovel a little for their attention?

They were really making out now, groping each other and stumbling in their eagerness. Mia finally pushed him away and lurched toward me. "Here," she said, and straddled my head.

"Kevin, why don't you suck my nipples while Cheyenne licks my pussy."

Without even being asked, I was enveloped in Mia's creamy pussy as Kevin sat astride my legs. I could feel his hard cock brush my knee as he leaned forward to take Mia's nipples into his mouth. I couldn't see a thing except her voluptuous ass covering my face. She was moaning softly, playing with her clit.

I pleasured her with my tongue as best I could, though it wasn't easy with her facing forward. I could tell that she and Kevin were still playing with each other from Kevin's groans and I wondered if they were just going to use me as their own personal sex furniture. At the same time, my mind was racing. Had they really both been loyal to me all summer? Had I ruined everything with this little revelation that I'd been dating them both?

Suddenly they murmured to each other and climbed off me. Thank god.

Mia lay down on me, smiling into my face. "Hi beautiful," she said and kissed me, tasting the sweetness of her own pussy.

Okay, she couldn't be that mad, judging by the way her lips moved on me. I'd always loved kissing Mia, and I melted beneath her now as her firm body covered mine. She opened her legs to line up with mine, leaving both of our pussies exposed. I glanced over her shoulder to see Kevin staring between our legs with a look of intense fascination. His gorgeous cock was thick and hard as he rolled on a condom. Then he climbed between our legs.

Please fuck me, I thought desperately, but it was Mia's pussy he pushed into. She stopped kissing me and got on all fours, furrowing her brow and groaning as Kevin fucked her. Once again I experienced the conflicting dual emotions of envying their sex, while enjoying the look of ecstasy on her face. Her beautiful breasts rocked over my face as Kevin drove in and out of her. He grinned at me—yep, he was loving every minute of this. They were both getting me back for two-timing them and there was nothing I could do but watch.

"Oh god," Kevin groaned. "I'm not going to last long...."

"Don't stop," Mia begged.

I watched Mia's face ripple with the pleasure of orgasm. The top of her breasts turned pink and the flush spread up to her face as she opened her mouth in a soundless cry of ecstasy, arching her back as Kevin pumped into her.

They were both so beautiful in their abandon. My clit ached to be touched. Yet as Kevin stood up with a grin, I could tell he wasn't quite done punishing me yet. His cock was still hard and he hadn't come yet; I could only hope that sex with me was next on his list. But I had a feeling he'd make me work for it.

Mia took a long drink of water from my bottle, then pulled up a lounge chair next to mine. "So," she said. "That's the guy you've been playing with all summer while I was at work. Who was the sex better with?"

No. That was the worst possible question she could ask me. Obviously she wanted to hear her name.

"It was awesome with both of you," I said cautiously, wondering if they could see how wet I was. "Mia—I really did think we were just having fun. I never would have—"

"Fun?" She slipped two fingers inside my clinging, creamy heat. She began to rub and stroke me from the inside, just how I liked it. "This kind of fun?" Her yellow-hazel eyes connected with mine.

I moaned and arched my back. "Yes," I groaned. "Oh please, don't stop."

Kevin laughed and moved closer, enjoying the show of Mia's pretty fingers sliding in and out of my cunt. "She's so easy, isn't she? I don't know if we should satisfy her just yet. I was pretty hurt when I found out about you two...."

"Ditto," Mia said, though she was still staring into my eyes. "I thought I meant something to her."

"You did! You do!" I pulled against my restraints, desperate for more of her fingers.

Mia leaned over, brushing her nipples against my lips. Her talented hands were playing my pussy like a violin, coaxing forth a thundering heat. I twisted helplessly in the lounge chair. "Do you want to come like this?" she whispered, softly pinching my clit until I cried out with pleasure. "Is that what you need?"

"Yes," I begged—and just as the thunder inside me began to roll toward a climax, she suddenly retreated with a naughty smile.

"Sorry."

Kevin replaced her, stroking his long, thick cock for my appreciative eyes. "So," he said. "You're probably hoping I'm going to let you come right about now."

I nodded eagerly. He smiled and wrapped his cock in a fresh condom. Was it really going to be this easy? Apparently so. Kevin climbed over my bound and naked body and effortlessly pushed his cock between my legs. Hot and hard as iron, his shaft filled all of me until I felt stretched wide. I moaned with gratitude and satisfaction.

And then he pulled out with that naughty grin. Dammit. Apparently this wasn't going to be as easy as I'd hoped.

"Kevin, please..." I twisted beneath him, trying to shake my breasts invitingly for his mouth. I couldn't touch myself or him, and everything from my clit to my nipples ached to be stimulated.

Kevin lightly slapped my breasts, and I arched my back again. "Fuck me," I begged.

He traced his swollen crown around my slit, teasing me until I was near tears. Rubbing it back and forth across my clit, he smiled as I twitched helplessly.

Then he drove deep into me again, making me scream with pleasure. Kevin began fucking me hard and fast now, driving in and out of me until his hips were a blur of rhythm. I gave into the white-hot bliss of being taken so smoothly and ruthlessly, my breasts bouncing in time with his thrusts.

Yet just as the liquid tension inside me built to a point, he pulled out again. With a devilish smile, he slapped the swollen head of his cock against my clit, over and over until my hips bucked up to meet him. "Please," I begged, "please." Then he shoved himself back inside me, thrusting fast and shallow for a few strokes, then driving all of the way in.

Bliss was filling my pussy, my every nerve alive with desire. Mia leaned over me, biting and sucking my stiff nipples until I thrashed in wordless pleasure. Then she kissed me, so deeply and demandingly that I knew I was forgiven. Whatever we had, whatever I had almost ruined, was still alive. Pure euphoria spread through my body and my pussy began to pulse around Kevin's shaft, squeezing him in the delirious throes of the hottest orgasm of my life. He uttered a low, long cry and held me tightly as he came, hips working furiously against me.

I sank into the lounge chair, luxuriating in the sleepy satisfaction filling my limbs. Mia knelt down to unlock my restraints and I sat up, rubbing my wrists. A cool breeze danced across my skin and I was surprised to see the sun setting in the west. How long had the three of us been out here? More importantly, could I persuade both of them to stay the night? And just maybe other nights once I had my own apartment again—the three of us together?

"So," I began tentatively. My voice was raspy from screaming.

"Once again I would like to apologize for not realizing you both thought we were exclusive—"

"Cheyenne, don't bother," Kevin said, waving my apology away. "It's okay. We never said we couldn't see other people."

"Ditto," Mia said. "It just hurt my feelings, realizing you had him on the side."

Kevin frowned. "Actually, you were the one on the side."

"No one was on the side!" I got up on shaky legs, reveling in the twilight breezes on my fevered, sticky skin. "Look, I start my new job tomorrow. I'm not going to have as much free time going forward—but tonight I've got the house to myself. Do you both want to stay over?"

Kevin and Mia eyed each other and smiled.

"I don't think we've punished her quite enough," Mia said. "What do you think?"

"Agreed," said Kevin. "I think Cheyenne's last night of freedom should be spent providing us with more sexual favors, just so we know that she's truly sorry."

Arm-in-arm, they led me into the house. I couldn't stop grinning. My last day and night of summer had turned out better than I could have dreamed. And I was pretty sure that after tonight, both of them would be open to turning our summer flings into an autumn romance for three.

FULL CIRCLE

Jade Melisande

Martina? Martina Lewis?"

Martina turned at the sound of her name to see the last person she had expected to find in the crowded conference hall.

"Hugh!" she exclaimed, grinning widely as he stepped forward and gave her a warm hug. She held him tight, then stepped back and put him at arm's length, looking him up and down just as he did her. He was of average height, built solidly, with white-blond crew-cut hair, a boyish grin and a dimple in his clean-shaven chin. He had always claimed he was going to grow a goatee to cover it up.

"I see you still haven't managed to grow facial hair," she teased, tweaking his dimple.

He flashed that grin she remembered so well. "You finally convinced me my dimple was an attention-getter, Marti. I decided to try out your theory." He winked. "It seems you may be right."

She gave a bark of laughter and shook her head. "Still the

same old Hugh," she said. She glanced around at the bustling conference hall. "I didn't realize you'd be here."

He shrugged. "It was sort of last minute. I knew you'd be here, though. Congratulations on your promotion."

Martini felt herself flush, chagrined that he had obviously followed her career while she had completely lost track of his. They had kept in touch for several months after last year's Expo, but their communications had gradually ebbed away, as work and life had drawn their attention from the brief fling they'd had. That and, for her, a new romance.

"You're with—"

"Digital Media," he supplied. "Based in Dallas."

Her eyes widened. "Of course!" she said, remembering now when the notification had come over LinkedIn of his appointment to director of marketing for the well-known media relations firm. She nodded thoughtfully. "Our Dallas office does some business with your firm," she said after a moment.

"Sure does," he replied. "And we hope to do more."

"Oh, then you probably know"—she had been about to say "my boyfriend," but caught herself just in time. Her and Jordan's relationship was not general knowledge in the organization, and she preferred to keep it that way, at least for the present. "Jordan Shaw," she amended. "Our VP of media relations? He's based in Dallas as well."

"I do at that," Hugh said, and she thought she caught a gleam of *something* in his eye, but before she could press further, she saw Jordan himself poking his head out the door of one of the meeting rooms. He glanced over at Martina and then at Hugh, who had turned to look in the direction of Martina's attention. After lifting a hand to Hugh, Jordan waved to Martina to hurry up. "They're starting," he mouthed.

Martina glanced around the hall, noting the crowds beginning to thin as people made their way into the various classes and seminars. She touched Hugh on the arm. "Gotta go," she said. "Will you be around for the mixer later? They're doing cocktails over in the aquarium, I hear. Rented out the whole place."

Hugh smiled and leaned in for a quick peck on her cheek. His scent was familiar, earthy and yet clean, like a forest after a rain. She felt her belly do an unexpected flip-flop and turned her head to see his laughing eyes boring into hers, as though he had read her reaction.

"Wouldn't miss it for the world," he said, turning away. "See you there."

A moment later Martina slipped into her seat next to Jordan. His citrusy scent was familiar, too, and for just a second she longed to run her hand over the ropy shoulder muscles she knew she would find beneath his tailored suit. They had agreed to keep their relationship private for the time being, but sometimes she just wanted to *claim* him. With his lanky frame and dark eyes and skin he was the exact opposite of Hugh, and yet she was deeply attracted to them both.

"I see you ran into Hugh," he whispered, as she opened her Notebook and prepared for the seminar. She glanced over at him, trying to gauge his reaction, but saw only curiosity in his face. She'd told him about the fling she'd had with Hugh at the conference last year—and that it had mostly died out when she and Jordan had started dating. They didn't have an exclusive arrangement—that would put too much of a strain on their long-distance relationship—but perhaps he'd react badly to having an ex-lover "in his face," so to speak. Still, Jordan had never been the jealous or insecure type, and in fact, had seemed to enjoy hearing about her sexual escapades. One night when they'd been drinking she'd even confessed to having had several threesomes, one with a married couple who were good friends of hers, one an on-and-off-again thing with a guy and his girlfriend in her twenties, and the other a one-night stand, with two men she'd met in a bar.

"You must think I'm a slut," she'd slurred tipsily. "But I like threeways. Hands everywhere, all that skin and warmth..."

Instead of deriding her, he'd pushed her back onto the couch and had demanded she give him details—as he slowly, deliberately, fucked her. Ever since then they had fantasized out loud with each other what it might be like to do that together, though they'd always left it at the fantasy stage.

"Yes," she whispered back, "he ran into me. He said you two know each other?"

Jordan nodded. "I'm the one that told him you'd be here," he said.

Martina snapped her gaze up from her computer screen and looked over at him. "You what?"

He didn't answer her, though, only grinned and stared straight ahead at the front of the room. "Shh," he admonished her. "The presentation is starting."

Three hours later Martina stood at the rail at the top of the aquarium, looking over at an immense fish tank that towered overhead, rising from the floor three stories below. If she tried, she could just see her reflection in the glass sides of it: long dark hair pulled into a braid on one side, a figure-hugging jersey dress in fire-engine red that matched her lipstick, nails and red stilettos. A little flashy, maybe, for a professional function, but this *was* an after-hours cocktail party, after all. It had nothing to do with the fact that she was meeting two men that she dearly wanted to impress.

Or so she told herself.

Lifting her glass of wine to her lips, she allowed herself to indulge in a momentary fantasy. She imagined meeting the two of *them* in that bar six years ago. Imagined flirting with them, teasing them, debating about which one she would go home with that night. And then, instead of making a choice between them, asking them *both* back to her place. She imagined kissing first one, and then, still with the taste of him in her mouth, turning to the other and kissing him. Back and forth, back and forth, until their tastes mingled and became one....

"Marti," Jordan said, materializing at her side. Martina jumped, blinking the fantasy away, and turned around to face him. Hugh stood a few feet behind him. She felt her face grow hot as she looked first at Jordan, then at Hugh, struggling to dispel the last vestiges of the fantasy. She saw their quizzical glance at each other.

"Hi," she said, a little breathlessly.

"You were a million miles away," Jordan said. "What were you thinking about?"

"I, um, nothing..." she managed.

Jordan laughed. "That's a whole lot of nothing!"

Hugh joined in on the laughter. "The last time I saw her look like that," he said, "I was making her tell me a dirty story."

Jordan leaned into her and put his mouth by her ear, but she knew, when he spoke, that Hugh could hear what he was saying. "So you told Hugh dirty stories, too, huh?" His breath was warm on her ear, his lips soft against the curve of her cheek. Martina turned her face away, acutely embarrassed. If possible, her cheeks grew even hotter.

"Jordan," she said, but was cut off when Hugh leaned in to her other side.

"I wonder if you told Jordan the same stories you told me," Hugh said. His mouth, too, was a whisper of warmth against her skin.

She felt Jordan's hand slide up the back side of her dress, felt Hugh's hand on the front of her thigh.

She struggled to catch her breath. She looked back and forth between them. Their mouths were so *damn* close—

"I think we need to take this somewhere else," Jordan said in her ear. He looked over at Hugh, and she saw Hugh nod back. She wondered if they could hear the pounding of her heart, feel the heat that suddenly flooded her, smell the scent of her spiking arousal. A sweet ache had started in her belly and spread out and down, until she felt a physical throbbing between her legs. Were they saying what she thought they were saying?

Afraid to ask for clarification, she merely allowed herself to be led silently between them out of the aquarium.

In the elevator there was a profound silence. Jordan's room was closer than hers, but hers had the better view, twenty-five stories up, looking out over the harbor. Her hands shook as she slid the room card into the reader. She did it wrong twice, until Jordan took it gently from her hand and put it in correctly, then pushed open the door and gestured for her to go in. She looked from his beloved, smiling eyes to Hugh's electric-blue ones, took a deep breath and stepped inside.

The door had barely closed behind them when she felt Jordan's arms around her, pulling her back against the wall of his chest.

"I love you, baby," he said in her ear. She turned in his arms to face him and found herself staring into Hugh's eyes over Jordan's shoulder. Hugh's arms were around Jordan's waist, his body pressed up against Jordan's back. His fingers lightly caressed her sides, and against her belly she could feel Jordan's erection beginning to stir. She pulled back just slightly, a tiny frown between her eyes.

"Jordan?"

He loosened one arm and turned slightly to pull Hugh into the circle. She watched, eyes wide, as Hugh leaned in, put a hand around the back of Jordan's neck, and then pulled him close to kiss him. Her heart beat a drum roll in her chest as she watched their mouths touch, their lips part and their tongues glide together briefly, before, with a sigh, they both turned to face her.

Her and Jordan's nonexclusivity was mutually agreed upon and had worked for them. They both acknowledged that long-distance relationships were hard to maintain, and had agreed that the added stricture of monogamy would only make it worse. Instead, having an open relationship had seemed to fuel their desire for each other when they were together, and listening to tales of each other's encounters had aroused them both. So she had known that Jordan had male lovers as well as female. But she had never confessed to him (*had she?*) that one of her most fervent fantasies was to see him with another man.

Jordan gathered her close and drew her to him for a slow, lingering kiss. His tongue tasted sweet, like the bourbon he enjoyed, and his lips, though soft, were demanding, insistent, against hers. She felt Hugh moving behind her, and then felt his body against hers, as it had been against Jordan's only moments before. Her groin clenched and she felt a wash of heat as she thought about Hugh's body pressed against Jordan's, about what it would be like to see them naked, skin against skin, light and dark with Hugh's cock nudging against Jordan's buttocks...

Her mind shut off there. It was too much to think about or even imagine.

Hugh's hands caressed her waist, encircling it, before drop-ping to her hips. He pulled her back against him, and she felt the evidence of his excitement pressed against her own buttocks. Jordan pulled his mouth away and began to nibble his way down her jaw to the hollow at the base of her throat. When she tipped her head back to give him better access, her head came to rest on Hugh's shoulder, and she felt Hugh's hand come up under her jaw, tilting her head back farther, holding her there for Jordan's ministrations.

She gasped and squirmed, and Hugh's arm tightened around her. Jordan's mouth was suddenly on hers again, drinking her, pulling her in until she gasped for air, and then he was kissing Hugh over her shoulder, with her sandwiched between them. She felt Jordan's hard chest against her own, his hands on her hips, scrunching the dress up and reaching for her bare skin beneath. She felt Hugh's cock twitch in his slacks where he was pressed against her and heard him moan into Jordan's mouth. Her head spun and she began clawing at the buttons on Jordan's shirt, needing to feel her skin against his. Jordan pulled his mouth away from Hugh's as he chuckled and captured her hands in his. Then with a deft movement he maneuvered them all back against the bed, which hit Hugh in the back of the knees. Hugh fell back with Martina on top of him and Jordan on top of her. They all laughed and flailed about, kicking off shoes and disentangling themselves from the heap they had fallen into. Now that her hands were free, Martina began to tear at their clothes in earnest. She couldn't bear to feel the barrier of cloth between them a moment longer, and desperately wanted to see them both, naked and lovely, lying in her bed.

And, oh, how she wanted to taste them. Every inch of them.

But they had other ideas. Hugh flipped her over so that she was on her back, and while he held her wrists, Jordan pulled the dress over her head. She lay there for a moment as they both stared at her in her lacy red panties and bra, and then their hands were everywhere, four of them, pulling at her clothing, caressing and touching and squeezing. Jordan's mouth trailed kisses down her belly as Hugh kissed her deeply for the first time since she had seen him, and she felt like she had gone to heaven. The look in their eyes when they pulled back and stared down at her nakedness was enough to send shivers up her spine: voracious, animalistic, *wanting.*

But she wanted, too.

When Jordan dipped his head lower, Martina found her voice. "No," she panted, "wait." They both paused, instant concern in Jordan's face.

"I—no, it's okay," she hastened to assure him. "I just...I want to see you. Both of you. Naked, with me."

Relieved grins wreathed both men's faces. "I think we can do that," Hugh said.

Martina hesitated a moment. "Can I watch...would you... undress each other?" She sensed that whatever-it-was between them was something they had been exploring already, and felt shy about asking, as though she was intruding into something intimate between them. But as desperately as she simply wanted to see and feel their bodies, she also wanted to see and feel what this *was* between them—and to be a part.

Jordan looked at Hugh, who gazed back at him with an open, trusting, look. She saw in that look that there *was* something else here, something deep. Her heart gave a little skip-hop.

Jordan leaned forward and kissed Hugh softly, then drew him to his feet next to the bed. Then, with infinite slowness, he began to undress him. As he unbuttoned and pulled Hugh's shirt off, he kissed his collarbone, then the bunched muscles of his shoulder, his forearm, the tendons at his wrist. Martina felt an ache in her chest as Hugh's fingers caressed Jordan's sharp cheekbone, and Jordan looked up to meet Hugh's eyes. Jordan placed his hands at Hugh's waist for a moment, then across his flat belly. His hand was so large and dark against Hugh's skin,

Martina was reminded of looking down and seeing his hand against *her* belly, and she shivered in vicarious pleasure. Then he was unbuttoning and pulling at Hugh's slacks. Hugh's cock was turgid against his underwear, a thick bulge beneath the material that Jordan's hand caressed with a featherlight touch. Martina saw Hugh shudder at that touch, but he did not move otherwise. She longed to drop to her knees in front of him and brush her face against the material, to feel his cock against her cheek, then gave a little gasp of pleasure as Jordan did just that, kneeling as he bent to remove Hugh's pants. Hugh moaned and brought his hands to Jordan's head, cupping the sides of it as Jordan buried his face against Hugh's groin.

Then Jordan was standing once more. She could hear Hugh's shallow breaths echoing her own. With a hand that visibly trembled, Hugh reached out and finished the job of unbuttoning Jordan's shirt that Martina had begun. He caressed the hard planes of Jordan's bare, hairless chest as he pulled the shirt back and off and ran his hands up Jordan's ropy biceps. Ever so slowly, he leaned in to take one of Jordan's nipples in his mouth. As his teeth grazed Jordan's flesh, Martina saw a shudder roll over Jordan and his eyes close. The room was so still that the sound of their breathing was clearly audible.

Martina felt the dampness between her legs spreading, felt her juices coating her inner thighs, felt her own excitement like a beat inside of her matching their synchronized breathing. When Hugh lowered himself to his knees in front of Jordan, pulling down Jordan's jeans and underwear as he did, Martina found her own mouth opening to the sight of Jordan's penis springing free. It was longer than Hugh's, but slimmer, and she longed to take it in her own mouth, to taste the salty precum she knew she would find at the tip. And then Hugh did just that, sliding his mouth around Jordan's cock and drawing him into the heat of his mouth all at once. They were so beautiful standing there, their male bodies so similar and yet so very different, it brought tears to her eyes.

And lust to her loins.

Martina could stand it no longer. She moaned and slid off the bed, then knelt at Jordan's feet, looking up at him in supplication. His eyes were closed, his hand around the back of Hugh's head as Hugh slid his mouth down the length of Jordan's shaft and back, but he must have sensed her movement because he opened his eyes and looked down at her.

"Baby," he said, his voice a hoarse sound in the still room. And that word was all she needed to know that she wasn't an intrusion. He wanted her to be a part of this thing that was between the two of them. As she leaned forward, he cupped a hand around the back of her neck as well, drawing her to him. Hugh's eyes opened as her face drew close to his. He turned his head slightly and their eyes met as their mouths and tongues touched and their breath mingled. Then she drew Jordan's cock into her mouth and felt Hugh's tongue sliding along the shaft after her mouth, lapping at her lips as he lapped at Jordan's cock and balls. Jordan's entire body trembled and then grew still as Martina worked at his cock, sliding her mouth up and down his shaft in the rhythm she knew he loved. His hand tightened on the back of her head and he groaned, thrusting deeply into her mouth. "Marti," he said, "Hugh—" and then nothing but a guttural gasp as he shuddered and spilled himself into her mouth. A moment later Hugh's mouth was next to hers and she kissed him with the salty taste of Jordan's semen clinging to her tongue.

They remained that way for a moment, before Jordan raised them both to their feet. "Come on," he said, his voice thready. "Your turn."

Martina didn't know if he meant her or Hugh, and she didn't care. She realized with sudden clarity that with the three of them, all of them would get "their turn." Giving and receiving, it was all part of the whole.

After that there were no more words, only hands and mouths and skin on skin.

Jordan lay on one side of her and Hugh, who had shed his underwear, lay on the other. She stroked and caressed their bodies in a kind of wonder. Her hand found Hugh's cock, remembered the thickness of it. She rolled to her side to pay him some individual attention, and felt Jordan behind her, already beginning to harden again. And then Jordan's hands were on her breasts and wandering farther down, mirroring her own hands on Hugh's body. Her legs parted and his fingers found her vulva and slipped between her soft folds. As he began to thrust them into her and push the heel of his palm against her clit the way she liked, she began to stroke Hugh in the same rhythm. Hugh's mouth found hers and he moaned into it. She felt his hands on her body and then felt them move across her to draw Jordan in, closer against her back. She felt Jordan's cock nestling against her backside and sliding back and forth in the wetness that had gathered there between her legs. They were moving in an undulating rhythm now, Jordan and Martina's hands moving as one, their three bodies rocking back and forth against one another. Martina felt the orgasm spiraling up through her as though it was a living thing, hot and liquid, and suddenly it was gushing, pouring out of her and through her, and she was pulling Hugh's orgasm from him, too, milking his semen from him as it spurted out all over her hand and into the space between their bodies. They both gasped, trying to catch their breath as Jordan's arms tightened around her convulsively and Hugh pulled them all into a tight, slippery hug. And then suddenly they were all laughing and hugging and kissing each other.

Much later, as Martina lay drowsing between the two of them, satiated and musing over the night's events, she knew that even if it never happened again, what had happened between them was something special, something she would treasure always.

But she had a feeling—a tiny, prescient notion—that it *would* happen again.

WHOSE ANNIVERSARY IS IT, ANYWAY?

Annabeth Leong

I eased the front door of our apartment shut behind me, still chilled and a little breathless from my early morning walk to the florist. The bouquet that I held made for some awkward fumbling as I tried to put away my purse and keys without making enough noise to wake someone up.

I paused to straighten and fuss over the bouquet. A dozen red-tipped yellow roses, symbolizing the unexpected turn toward romance that our friendship had taken four years ago. Smiling to myself, I crept toward the bed.

Kenzie still slept, all four of her limbs out flung as if she suffered a particularly pleasurable torment. The heat of the blankets had made her sweat a little, and a few matted locks of her blonde hair stuck to her forehead. A slight frown creased her face into the familiar expression she took on while concentrating—which covered everything from balancing her checkbook to applying precise and fearsome pleasure to my dripping pussy. It turned me on just to look at her, like it always had, even long before I learned to admit it.

I hid the flowers behind my back and leaned forward to drop a kiss at her temple. "Sweetheart," I crooned. "Love. Happy anniversary."

Hazel eyes blinked open. Kenzie groaned and struggled, pressing her palms to her eyelids, the corners of her mouth, the sides of her head. "Mara?" Her voice sounded small, as if it had to travel a very long distance to reach me from her dreams.

Affection overwhelmed me. I dropped the flowers next to the bed and lay down next to her, the mattress dropping under my weight. She leaned into me, burying her face between my breasts as if she could hide from the morning there. I wrapped her in my arms, rocked her like the precious love that she was and rained kisses into her damp hair. "I got you flowers."

She sighed. "I love you, Mara." Kenzie tipped her head back to look me in the eye, and I couldn't resist the pale expanse of her exposed neck. When we first got together, I could spend hours just stroking all her soft skin, and the impulse had never really gone away. I rubbed my lips up the side of her neck, not kissing so much as feeling her with an exquisitely sensitive part of me.

Kenzie moaned, and I would have lost myself in her then except for a new groan from the other side of the bed, this one deeper and more of a growl. "You got her flowers?" Dylan always sounded grouchy in the morning, so I didn't take his tone of voice too personally. I smiled hello at him when he sat up.

He scowled, his blue eyes even more piercing than usual. The streaks of gray at his temples made him look authoritative and professorial even when half-naked and splotched red from pillows. "What the hell's the occasion?"

Kenzie, seemingly oblivious to his mood, turned to him and

smiled beatifically. She twined willowy arms around his neck and gave him a deep, languid kiss with lots of tongue—a hell of a lot more than I'd gotten so far, and I'd been the one to slip out of the bed early to try to make the day special. I tried not to begrudge him the moment.

Dylan stroked Kenzie's back absently, continuing to hold her after she pulled back from the kiss. I sighed and scooted closer to them, leaving the flowers on the floor for the time being. Their bodies felt almost uncomfortably warm after the cool air outside, but now I wanted to be included in the moment.

Kenzie somehow managed to make herself melt into both of us. She lay across our laps, accepting our caresses with the divine innocence that had always prevented her presence from coming between me and my husband.

Dylan touched my hair, which I had already put up in a French twist. His fingers slid down to my earlobe, closing around one of the pearl earrings he'd given me. The calloused pads of his fingertips scraped my cheek as he traced the line of the blush I'd applied before going out. His eyes narrowed with the respect and challenge that had always brought us together.

He shook his head. "You are miles ahead of me this morning, Mara."

I kissed the palm of his hand quickly, acknowledging the compliment that came folded within his accusing tone.

His face softened for just a moment, the severe lines of his lips slipping into something more sensual. Then Kenzie stretched and offered an explanation for the flowers. "Today is our anniversary."

"What?" Dylan snatched his hand away from me and raked it through his hair. "I could swear our anniversary is June twenty-third. I've got the wrong date?"

"No," Kenzie said in her most playful voice, giggling a little.

She rolled onto her stomach, tugged the blanket off Dylan's legs and planted a kiss on his thigh. He could pretend to panic about anniversaries all he wanted—his erection rose beside her head, strong and unmistakable. He couldn't be feeling too much pain.

I filled in the rest of the detail. "It's my anniversary with Kenzie. We had our first date on this night four years ago, back when you and I had just agreed to open up our marriage."

"Oh my god. You celebrate separate anniversaries?"

Kenzie laughed and the glance she slanted up at Dylan contained mischief along with her usual sweetness. "We celebrate all kinds of anniversaries. First date. First kiss—which was not the same day. First time we said we loved each other. First time we had sex. I didn't put out for Mara for four whole months, you know. Not like I did for you."

"The night we met," Dylan whispered, and a stab of jealous arousal flashed through me as I saw the memory flicker across his face. I'd brought Kenzie home to meet him because I thought she was everything we'd both been looking for. I thought Dylan would fall as madly in love with her as I had, and he did. Before Kenzie, I'd wondered if opening our marriage was merely a precursor to drifting apart and eventually separating. When I realized I was willing to share Kenzie with Dylan—that I wanted to because I thought she would delight him—I knew he and I really had something together.

So I'd only been a little envious of the lightning that crackled between them when they met.

That first night, I sat quietly at the dining room table while Dylan revealed a dominant side I'd only ever glimpsed. Within thirty minutes, he had ordered her to reach under the table and touch herself through her dress. The command surprised me, but watching my sweet, demure Kenzie obey shocked me even more.

"Pull up the dress," Dylan had said, his voice low and hard and self-satisfied. "Feel the cushion against your bare legs. Is your pussy wet?"

"God, yes," Kenzie had answered, shooting me a look of apology.

"It's okay, sweetheart," I soothed her.

"Give me your panties," Dylan ordered next. Kenzie barely blinked as she slipped off the scrap of cotton she wore and passed it across the table. I blinked, barely recognizing my lover or my husband.

The scene didn't take long to progress. Soon, Kenzie knelt beside Dylan's chair, her head in his lap as he wrapped her hair around his hand and pulled her face toward his hard cock. As her lips stretched around him, Dylan let me see the ecstasy in his eyes, then mouthed, "You okay?"

I swallowed and nodded, shifting in my chair from the discomfort of my arousal. I knew that cock, understood exactly how it would feel pressing against the back of Kenzie's throat, and exactly what she would smell with her nose buried in Dylan's pubic hair. I also knew that mouth, had intimately experienced the sweet, warm softness of Kenzie's tongue, the depth of focus she applied to pleasing a lover, the yielding heat of the insides of her cheeks and the way she could scrape her teeth just so against the most sensitive places and make the gesture feel delicious.

That was the first time I really saw how being with two people at once could intensify my pleasure, even when they paid attention to each other instead of me.

"That was January twenty-seventh," I told them now. "The first night I brought Kenzie here. June twenty-third was when she moved in."

Dylan nodded. "Right. Our anniversary. June twenty-third, when all three of us got together and committed to one another."

Kenzie lifted her head and smiled like the cat that ate the canary. "We'll definitely celebrate June twenty-third when it comes around, all three of us. That was just over a year after Mara and I started dating. That anniversary is May fifteenth. Today. So today is my day with Mara, and January twenty-seventh is my day with you, and your and Mara's anniversary is...?"

"We got married October sixth," Dylan said automatically. "I don't know how you keep the rest of that straight."

Kenzie gave a pleased smile, then kissed the tip of his cock, where I noticed a bead of precum.

I couldn't take it anymore and gave a little growl. "So if today's our day, why is he getting all my anniversary kisses?"

Kenzie lifted her head, but Dylan stopped her before she could turn back to me. "I don't see why we can't all share," he said. "That's what this is all about, right?" He quirked a grin. "Besides, aren't you going to celebrate the first time you saw her nipples or something a couple of months from now? I think you'll get your chance."

I glanced toward the flowers and frowned. Honestly, I had expected Dylan to sleep a little longer. I'd pictured a romantic breakfast, just me and Kenzie, full of lots of cute reminiscences about the restaurant I'd taken her to for that first date. I could summon the nervousness I'd felt around her as if it was yesterday. She was the most beautiful woman I'd ever seen, and it had taken so long for me to realize I wanted to be with her, not be her.

When I realized I wanted to have sex with Kenzie, I felt so much relief. I could look in the mirror and see someone bigger, browner and more irritable than her and be fine with it. I didn't need to see her face in the mirror—I needed to see it gazing up at me from between my legs. I didn't need to have a complexion as perfect as hers—I just needed to be able to kiss and stroke her skin.

On our first date, I ached with the sort of awkward sexual awareness I hadn't felt since puberty. I'd stammered and lapsed into long silences. I'd asked inane questions. And Kenzie had given me her sunny, saintly smile through the entire painful meal, sipping her mint ice tea with relish that amazed me considering that I could barely taste the food in front of me. At the end of the meal, she'd leaned in close and asked in a conspiratorial whisper, "Are you trying to get in my pants, Mara?"

Until that moment, I hadn't realized I'd failed to be clear that we were on a date. Something about her tone of voice made what could have been a moment of humiliation turn out okay. She spoke like she was on the same side as me.

We left the restaurant and took a long walk and talked about every detail of our sexual histories. We laughed and groaned in appropriate places, and sometimes we drifted into tense, wanting silences. I was too afraid to touch her that night, even though I thought she might have let me. Still, by the time I dropped her off at her house, the scent of my arousal filled the entire car. I pulled over a block from her house, unzipped my jeans and masturbated with noisy desperation, rocking against my fingers with no care for how it would look if someone saw me there. I grunted and moaned and screamed louder than I normally did fucking.

Then I licked my juices off my fingers, imagined they were Kenzie's and got so horny at the thought that I had to do it all over again.

Dylan brought me back to the present with a rough kiss, reminding me of his presence in the room, and the relationship, with the gruff force that had always made me love him. I relented, opening my mouth for him and accepting his hard, probing tongue. He must have been horny, because he quickly followed with pinches to my nipples and a groping hand working its way under my ass. He grabbed handfuls of my curves through the slacks I'd put on before heading out to the florist.

For all that my mind had been on Kenzie all morning, Dylan got through to me. He squeezed me tighter and pushed his tongue deeper until I gasped into his mouth.

"It's Saturday," he said when he released me. "I want us all to be together, at least for the morning. Can you take her out to dinner or something later? Please?"

I glanced at Kenzie, then back at Dylan. She frowned just a little, then shook her head. "Mara and I need a few minutes of privacy first," she said in a tone of voice that brooked no argument. "Then, if you really want to get involved, you can help me fuck her."

I smiled with gratitude, glad that Kenzie knew me so well. It would have been a little hard for me to state the facts of my feelings so bluntly, and it was a relief to have that done for me.

Dylan sighed. "If I'm helping you fuck Mara, that means I shouldn't take care of myself in the shower. So unfair."

She slapped him lightly. "Don't whine. We'll go to the kitchen and be back in five minutes. You can nap in the meantime. You will barely miss us."

He gestured toward his erection. "So untrue."

Kenzie grinned, then jumped out of bed and snatched the flowers up off the floor. The sheets fell away from her gloriously, revealing every soft, pale curve and her candy-pink nipples, huge and hard compared with her tight, small breasts.

Dylan nudged me. "Don't just sit there with a slack jaw. I think she wants you to go with her."

Even four years into the relationship, I still sometimes couldn't believe that this woman would be looking at me with a soft glow in her eyes, or that my husband would push me to go after her. I smiled at them both and followed Kenzie into the kitchen.

"Thank you for the flowers," she said when we got there, then gave me a kiss that made me melt. I wanted to take it much farther, push her back against the table, spread her legs and make a breakfast of her. Knowing our limited time, I restrained myself.

Kenzie unwrapped the flowers and transferred them to a vase. Her slim fingers moved with quick expertise, trimming and arranging. I never got enough of watching her.

"What do you think of Dylan being with us this morning?" Kenzie asked after a minute.

I shrugged. "I had planned an anniversary with you, but it doesn't seem fair to leave him out."

"I think he's torn. He wants to respect the relationship the two of us have with each other—that's why he mentioned that you should take me out to dinner—but he also wants to know that you still love him, too."

"You were the one he was kissing," I said, beginning to feel embarrassed about my petulance.

Kenzie set the flowers in their vase and stepped in close to me. The sight of her naked body pressed against my clothed one inflamed me. I wanted to put my hands all over her.

She wrapped her arms around me and leaned her head against my chest. "Sometimes, he loves you through me."

"Huh?"

"He and I understand something that you don't."

"Of course. We all have our own—"

She stopped me with a finger over my lips. Kenzie tipped her head back and gave me a sly smile. "Shh. I'm going to tell you what it is." She sighed. "You know that we love you. You were with him first, and he fell in love with you, and then you were with me, and I fell in love with you. For me and him, there's always this little fear that you don't love us back. That maybe you love him more because you loved him first. Or that you love me more because—I don't know exactly how he thinks about it. I think Dylan's having a hard time watching us have an anniversary that doesn't include him. He needs to be reassured."

"Of course I love him, too," I protested. Then, softly, I admitted the truth. "I just don't want to share you right now. Not this morning."

"We're going to make you feel so good, Mara," Kenzie replied in a teasing voice.

I sighed. "This is hard."

"Of course it is. Marriage is hard."

"This isn't exactly a normal marriage."

"That doesn't make it easy."

"How do you feel about Dylan being with us?"

Kenzie grinned wickedly. "I figure he can help us celebrate. I have a plan."

I gave a nervous laugh in reply, then accepted her long hug. "You're so smart about us. How the hell did we get along before you came here?"

"You'd be divorced by now if not for me."

She said it in her usual sunny tones, but I did sometimes fear it was true. I have heard people say that two is a stable unit and three introduces instability. For all that I felt the back-and-forth tugs of jealousy since our marriage had become a threesome, I knew Kenzie had the opposite effect. She stabilized my relationship with Dylan. I kissed her cheek. "Okay, I'll place myself in your hands."

"Good."

She led me back to the bedroom, where Dylan waited. Impatiently, I might add. He lay in bed jerking off slowly, his hand moving up and down on his shaft with exquisite languor.

"Enough," Kenzie said. "Mara, you should take off your clothes and lie down next to him."

I blinked, unused to her being so dominant. Still, I did as she told me, noticing the way Dylan raked a hungry glance over my bared nipples. There was something else on his face, too, something beyond lust. I wondered if Kenzie had been right in her assessment, that he'd started horning in on our morning because he needed reassurance from me.

Kenzie curled her body on the bed at our feet. "Do you know the hottest thing you told me on our first date?"

Dylan looked up with interest. My cheeks heated. I could think of lots of candidates, but nothing that stood out as an obvious winner.

She smiled, then answered her own question. "It was about the first kiss you two had. Dylan, do you remember how it went?"

"Of course I do." He sounded grouchy as hell. That told me more than anything else that Kenzie had been right—he always covered vulnerable feelings with irritation, not unlike my own habits. I wondered if we'd picked that pattern up from each other, or if it had been part of the similarity that had initially drawn us to each other.

"It made me so wet to hear about it," she said naughtily. "I want to see it."

"Well," Dylan said, warming up to the scenario. "We actually looked a lot like this, except younger." His hand crept under the covers and found mine. I let him take it, emotion stirring in my chest. "It was morning, and we were both naked. We'd fucked the night before—and I mean fucked—we didn't just knock over a chair on the way to the bed, we overturned a table. We hadn't kissed yet, partly because she wouldn't let me do it, and partly because I'd spent most of our time in bed shoving her face into the pillow while I pounded her from behind."

I had to laugh, squeezing his hand. "Wow, you make it sound so romantic."

"It was the hottest sex of my life. That's romantic to me." He turned back to Kenzie and continued his story. "Anyway, I woke up and Mara was already awake, watching me. There was this sweetness on her face that spoke volumes."

"I was not sweet."

He smiled indulgently. "That's what you tried to make me think at the time, too. As soon as you saw my eyes had opened, your face smoothed right out and got all inscrutable. Before I thought about what I was doing, I reached out to you. I wanted what I'd seen before. So I kissed you. Like this."

Dylan touched my cheek and looked deep into my eyes until I wanted to squirm. He'd been right then, and he was right now. I couldn't hold back from him when he really searched me this way. After a long moment, I felt myself opening to him, thawing. I might never have felt the sort of all-encompassing adoration for him that I did for Kenzie, but somehow he could touch me in a very deep place that no one else could reach.

I tried to look away, to keep him out, but he stroked his fingers upward until they rested just beside my eyes and waited until, slowly, I returned my gaze to him.

The air between us trembled and ached. Then he leaned forward and brushed his lips against mine, so softly that I could barely feel them. Once. Twice. Three times. Until he made me think he'd go on like that forever without ever giving me the full force of the promise that had formed between us.

I couldn't help myself anymore, and grabbed the back of his head and pulled him in. The invitation set off a chain reaction. His tongue in my mouth, his body rolling onto mine, his every limb entwined with mine. Hands and arms and feet and legs, until I couldn't tell where he ended and I began.

Dylan pulled back very slightly and met my eyes again, his face asking the same question that it had so long ago. And I gave the same answer. "Yes," I whispered, and spread my legs just a little wider, enough to make his cock slip into me.

His cock inside me felt different now than almost every other time.

Dylan was right to use the word "fuck" when he told the story to Kenzie. He and I liked to get nasty together. We liked to shock, one-upping each other by moving faster, or harder. He'd fold my legs up against my chest and bang the head of his cock against my G-spot until I begged for mercy. Then I'd roll him over and turn my back to him and jump on top in reverse cowgirl and make him slide a finger up my ass while I rode him at top speed.

This time, though, the posturing fell away, like it had that first morning together. We lay united, caught in sure, simple rhythm. My body squeezed around his body. Our skin reached the same temperature. We slid smoothly together, frictionless thanks to sweat and arousal. The other stuff we did was fun, but this was...complete.

Then a hand insinuated itself between our bodies and I remembered Kenzie. Our anniversary. Weird guilt flashed through me for getting so involved with my husband that I forgot she was sitting there.

Kenzie didn't seem disturbed in the least, though. She sat on her heels beside us, and slid her arms into a weird embrace. Her right hand found my clit. Her left arm snaked through the tangle of our legs and rested on my thigh. Dylan gasped, and I figured she'd found either his balls or his asshole.

She touched me slowly but with precision. She didn't change the rhythm Dylan and I had established. She enhanced it.

His gaze drilled into me. I mouthed, "You okay?"

He smiled and dropped his head beside mine. "I love you," I whispered into his ear, then savored the words we rarely spoke aloud.

Kenzie's finger never left my clit, her slow, sweet circles lifting me higher with sureness and solidity. Her hand. His cock. I gave in to them both with a low groan and a ripple that reached every hidden place of my body. I cried out and rocked, wrestling with pleasure that felt like more than I could handle.

The release of orgasm wasn't enough. I had to share what I felt. I nudged Dylan until he made a little space between our bodies, then tugged Kenzie so she released the intimate hold she had on us both. I pulled her up to my face, needing to taste her.

Her cunt flowed into my mouth as Dylan continued to fuck me slowly. She smelled like the ocean, and her juices poured onto my tongue with the bracing snap of a salty, windy day. I licked her, wanting to please her, to make up to her for things I couldn't even articulate. I thought maybe love always felt like this, like wanting to give more than I knew how to give.

I brought up a finger and slipped it into her, smiling against her clit when her cunt muscles gripped me tight. Her moan above me sounded muffled, and I glanced up in surprise to see her locked into a hungry kiss with Dylan.

I didn't know how we'd gotten lucky enough to all find each other, to love each other in this deep, complicated way. A warm glow filled me, and I gave myself up to the sensation of him, of her, knowing each of them experienced something that overlapped with what I felt but also differed.

Dylan made love to me the way he had the day our first fuck turned into something more, but now Kenzie had become part of it, too. I moved my mouth from her cunt for just a moment. "Happy anniversary," I said, and they both smiled.

LIMITS OF ENDURANCE

Ariel Graham

W e're not going to die up here."

The declaration has echoed through Cassidy's head for the last two hours, and it's looking less true with every second that ticks by.

She's tiring rapidly, partly because of the cold, partly because she's hungry. Partly, probably, because Max and Cody move so damn fast.

She can't ask them to slow down. They can't slow down. It's a stupid situation, absurd, the kind of thing she rolls her eyes at when it comes on the nightly news or she sees it in a newspaper. She pants after both men, sides aching, quadriceps and hamstrings screaming, step after step after step.

Every year articles appear and news segments broadcast how hikers on Mount Hood have gotten lost. They left at ten a.m. and haven't come back. They were trained. They weren't trained. They had cell phones. Or not. The day was, routinely, beautiful when they left. Only after they got up there into the scenic reaches of the glaciers and looked down at all the trees did the storm clouds blow in. But now with the unprecedented weather, it's freezing at seven thousand or eight thousand feet or however far they must have gotten, and no one can remember if the hikers carried outdoor gear or matches or flares or any smidgen of common sense.

"We're not going to die up here."

Beside her, having dropped back to her speed, Cody says, "No, we're not."

Cassidy looks up, surprised. "Did I say that aloud?"

Above them, Max, standing with hands on hips, chest heaving, says, "For the last half hour." He stares at her for a second, and then grins. "Hey, at least it's positive."

The sun glints out for a minute, just a tease from behind snow clouds that keep ripping open and spilling down on them, and Cassidy gets a good look at his face, the streaky dirt covering his dark, one-eighth-American-Indian tan and curling black hair. He's stocky and broad and faster than he looks like he should be. She should know—she's been trying to catch up to him all day and she's not short. She's tall, lanky and in nowhere near as good a condition as she thought she was before she started hiking with her two best friends.

"Next time I'll go with girls," she says without thinking.

Beside her, golden Cody, lean, athletic, grinning, says, "Why? Do you think girls have a better sense of direction?"

She grins back, despite the fear crawling through her veins. Last time she checked her watch it was after six. At midsummer the days are long, but the sun will set eventually. For that matter, at midsummer it shouldn't be snowing.

"At least girls wouldn't have dropped the compass in the runoff," she says, but lightly. Before she can follow up, Max says, "If I told you which way north was, would that help?"

"Do you know?" she counters.

"Based on the sun setting, yeah, I have a clue."

She thinks of that too late. "Yeah, me too."

"Doesn't matter." Cody has stepped away from them, scanning the mountain around them. It seems impossible to get lost on a mountain—getting off of it should mean going down—but every time they try to go down they're trapped by something in their way. Then the storm blew up, icing skin, making it harder and harder to keep moving when keeping moving is exactly what they need to do.

Cody speaks again first. "I think we have about three more hours of workable daylight," he says.

This time Cassidy keeps her thoughts to herself when her internal voice substitutes "stumble-able" for "workable." Because none of them are doing very well. Max twisted an ankle some time back and he hasn't admitted it; Cody is clearly hurting from some injury, too. Cassidy hurts all over and would admit it freely if it would help. Right now she wants to hold another meeting of the minds—a "So what do we do now?"—only it won't help. They have very few options. They have their sweatshirts, but they're wearing shorts. No ponchos. No tents. Matches, but no hand warmers.

Cody, for no reason she can imagine, is carrying one two-person sleeping bag wrapped in a ground sheet and hanging from his pack. They have water and food in daypacks, enough to get them each through about three days, but that's not the issue. The issue is the snow that starts falling again, thicker than ever even as Cassidy gazes at the valley floor they can't get back down to. Directly under them is a broken field of rocks that came down in some avalanche or another. They tried clamoring down them, but the rocks aren't set—they tumbled and started a mini-slide and that's when Max twisted his ankle. To one side there's a creek caused by snowmelt runoff, and after so many hours, they are all reaching the limits of their endurance.

The view of the valley and the city beyond is spectacular. Cassidy almost loses herself, forgetting the panic gnawing at her for just an instant. She jolts back when Cody says, "Up there!" and points.

We don't want to go up, Cassidy thinks automatically. They want to go *down*. She wants to go *home* and see her best friends on another day. A dry, hot, stay-inside-and-watch-movies kind of day. But Cody is pointing up the mountain and when she squints in the direction he's gesturing, Cassidy sees an opening on the side. It's not much—it's a *cave*, her inner girl protests— but it's at least out of the snow.

The snowfall changes then, as the sun breaks free from the clouds. It's too far down the sky now to produce much warmth—it's verging on seven thirty—but it's enough to change the summer snow to sleet.

They are soaked in an instant.

"Up!" Max says without hesitation. "Even if it's shallow, it's shelter. We have to get out of this."

It takes fifteen minutes to reach the cave. It's farther away than it looks, and the sleet is blinding and the trail studded with rocks and holes leading to animal burrows.

I'm never going hiking again, Cassidy swears to herself as they reach the edge of the cave.

"Anyone remember what you're supposed to do to make sure there's no one home?" Cody asks.

Cassidy blinks, thinking he's gone mad, then feels a chill more intense than even the weather when she understands he means mountain lion or coyote or bears or whatever Mount Hood is home to that might live in a cave and not welcome visitors.

Max shrugs. "I don't know, but I suggest shouting."

Cassidy stares at him and he manages to shrug again, looking almost nonchalant, but she can see the sickly pale under his tan. He's hurting, cold and tired as the rest of them. They have to get inside.

"Hey!" she shouts and the other two join her instantly, shouting for lions, tigers, bears and mostly making noise because the animals aren't really going to respond to "Anybody home?" until they fall silent about the same time and look at each other in the sleet.

"Come on," Cody says.

The ground is dry and rocky under the overhang. There's no evidence of animals, and the cave only goes back about eight feet, ending in blunt rock wall. Nowhere for animals to hide, they see now, but the floor is covered in pine needles and they can make their own den. Cassidy is so tired that even the rocks look comfortable. She sinks down onto one of the large rocks inside the cave with a sigh. "Would one of you draw me a hot bath?" she asks in her most diva voice.

"Got a pen?" Max asks, and she opens her eyes enough to roll them at him.

"Right," Cody says. "Anyone remember how to build a fire in a cave so we don't all die of smoke inhalation?" He looks at them expectantly.

"Aren't you the happy camper," Max says.

"Not really, or I would know all this."

"I remember," Cassidy says, putting away her cell phone again. No signal. There's been no signal for any of them all day. She sighs and sets about making the fire.

The fire smoldered at first, then caught, about the time the light started fading faster from the sky and the snow came down again, lazily but with a wind. At first the flames felt good and Cassidy held her hands out toward them. Then the chills caught her. Her teeth began to chatter. She giggled, then realized she couldn't make them stop. Her stomach muscles started to spasm with cold. Deep shudders rippled through her.

"Cassidy!"

She heard Max's voice, from a distance, it seemed. She wrapped her arms around herself, but her clothes were clammy and wet. Shivering uncontrollably, she started to cry, her breath coming unevenly.

Cody grabbed her, pulled her a little back from the fire as she shook. "Shit, Cass, these clothes are soaked."

"So...so...so are yours," she managed.

Cody didn't bother to answer. "We need to get her out of these. Max, get the sleeping bag open."

But Max had already unrolled it, laying the plastic it had been wrapped in under it and smoothing it closer to the fire. He joined Cody, taking Cassidy's other side. "Put your arms up, Cass," he said, trying to peel the sweatshirt off of her and Cassidy, limp from the cold, felt her cheeks flame with heat.

"You can't," she started. In her mind she heard her father: *Why can't you be friends with girls?* And her mother, then, trying to mollify: *At least they're just friends*, and then, to Cassidy: *Right?*

They couldn't undress her. They were friends. The three of them.

"Please," she said.

"Don't be an idiot," Cody said and grabbed her hand, pulling her arm out from her body at the same time he pulled the sodden sleeve of her sweatshirt out and shoved her arm back into the garment. The gesture smacked of someone who'd had long practice with younger siblings and was better than whatever Max was doing with her right arm.

They managed to tangle her in the sweatshirt briefly, blinding her with the shirt over her head, clammy wetness in her face. While Max tugged at that, Cody pulled her T-shirt up and got her arms out and by now she was shaking too hard to either help or hinder them. She protested when he unhooked her bra, but even as Max stripped the sweatshirt over her head finally she felt the heat of the fire on her skin, the cold on her back, and tried to get her boots off because her feet ached with cold.

"You're just getting in the way," Cody said, and brushed her hands aside. Boots came off easily, socks followed, sodden things, and then her shorts and Cassidy, half horrified, half thrilled with the heat, let them do what they needed to do to help her. She huddled by the fire as Max and Cody made short work of stripping off their clothes. She hadn't expected that, hadn't been coherent enough to even think about it, but it made sense.

The sleeping bag was made for two. Max unzipped it all the way and fanned it out like a cloak until Cody took one side and together they sat down beside Cassidy, bringing the sleeping bag around her.

For the first time in hours the chill inside her started to recede.

We're not going to die up here.

She didn't think she said it aloud.

The night deepened, pitch black with no stars, but the snow finally stopped.

"Tomorrow the snow should melt off early," Cody said.

"Its June twenty-second tomorrow," Cassidy said. "Isn't it illegal for it to be snowing anyway?"

"Yes, but the gods never listen," Max said so seriously they both turned and stared at him.

"Gods?" Cody hazarded.

"Illegal?" Max replied.

Cassidy laughed.

"That's a good sound," Max said, and she became subdued again without meaning to. With the sleeping bag over her shoulders, she was somewhat covered but still hideously aware she was naked. Their clothes were spread on rocks on the other side of the fire but she didn't think they'd be dry even by morning and wasn't looking forward to putting them back on.

"So how did three reasonably intelligent people end up a cautionary tale on the side of a mountain in a snowstorm?" she asked them and blushed when Max glanced quickly at her and away again.

"Cautionary tales are usually postmortem," he said. "We're just—what?"

He looked over her head at Cody.

"A 'don't be idiots' tale? 'How the idiots survived themselves'?"

"As long as we survive," Cassidy said, and shivered again.

"Right," Cody said. "Anyone for ghost stories?"

It was nearing midnight when the mist started up. Whether that meant the temperature had gone up or down none of them knew or could agree. What they did know was the moisture threatened their fire, and the temperature in their cave dropped again. Cassidy started to shiver again and couldn't stop.

They'd all been half dozing before this most recent temperature change. Now they huddled there, three people keeping polite space between naked bodies under an open sleeping bag.

It almost wasn't working anymore. The fire sputtered, didn't go out, but didn't want to blaze in the damp. They had fuel—

there were plenty of pine needles—but they were all shivering again, unable to get warm.

We're *not*, Cassidy thought, fierce, but unwilling to finish the thought. Even thinking of death now scared her. Thoughts ran through her head, full of things she didn't really know and couldn't remember properly, like core body temperature and hypothermia and how many cautionary tales about idiots lost in the mountains and caught in freak snowstorms there were every year.

How many were true.

How often said idiots survived.

"Hate to get fresh," Cody said, jolting Cassidy out of her thoughts. "But we need to share body heat."

By unspoken agreement, Max moved also, the two of them pressing up against Cassidy, their arms going around her and her arms reaching to circle their legs.

I'm sure my parents would love to know about me and my friends right now, Cassidy thought, and shifted as her arm cramped with shivers. She pulled it back, trying to turn her upper body fractionally, and brushed Cody's cock with her forearm.

Cassidy stilled instantly, blush sending hot chills through her that instantly iced.

"Oh my god, I'm so sorry, Code," she said, trying to look at anything but either of the men. A split second later she realized that Cody was hard, very hard, and his breathing had changed.

"No problem," he said, his voice thick. "I liked it."

Cassidy giggled unexpectedly, turned toward him, and Max's right arm, the one circling over the front of her body, rode hard over her nipples.

"Um," Max said, but Cassidy was laughing too hard then to

get out more than, "No problem," before she started laughing again.

"She liked it," Cody finished for her, and Cassidy stopped laughing as if she never had been.

If she had given herself time to think, probably she would have stopped. But the only thoughts in her mind were the warmth of flesh. Where they touched her was warm and where they didn't touch her was cold. And she absolutely needed to get warm.

She reached for both of them, not looking at either, wanting and afraid and scared of the night, the snow and the cold.

Max was every bit as hard as Cody, with a thicker, shorter cock that leapt in her hand as she closed her fingers around it. Cody was huge, long and not as thick, but hard and beaded with want. Cassidy ran her hands lightly along their lengths and started slightly when Max pulled his arms back, his right still crossed over her chest but now rubbing her breasts, tugging and rolling her nipples. Electric shocks surged down to her cunt. Her clit hardened like her nipples but not from cold. Max's left hand rubbed the small of her back, just above her ass, bumping into Cody's hand. Cody, his head back, eyes probably closed, reached to Cassidy's lap, gentled her thighs apart and began to stroke fingers down into her swollen, wet folds. Cassidy stiffened again, rolled her hips toward him, opened her legs.

A sudden up-kick of wind made the fire flare and die back. Snow blew into their cave, just enough to coat them before melting off. Both men shifted out of her grasp, released their holds on her, and Cassidy felt the shuddering start again. She started to say something, started to say they couldn't stay there, maybe they should get dressed and take their chances going down the mountain, but Max stood suddenly, leaving the sleeping bag around the other two, and moved behind the rocks where they sat, shaking out the ground sheet.

Cassidy turned, briefly looked at Max's strong, broad shoulders, tight ass, the dark hair that curled down his chest, leading lower, a path down to the cock she'd just held in her hand. She flushed again when Cody stood, leaving her under the sleeping bag, moving to help Max shake out the ground sheet. Cody was taller, slimmer, with long lines of muscles and blond hair that curled from the dampness. He was clean shaven, Cassidy noticed, and then blushed and shivered so hard she made an involuntary noise.

"Cass," Cody said, catching her as she started to fall backward off the rock she had perched on. He pulled her to her feet, and the sleeping bag fell away from her. Max caught it, brought it with him as he followed the other two. A moment of confusion while Cassidy's brain and body couldn't quite decide what she wanted them to do and then she was curling up on the ground sheet, Max and Cody following her down, the sleeping bag covering the three of them.

"We have to get her warm," Cody said over her head. He was spooned up against Cassidy's back, Max was curled into her, his arms around her, his not-that-warm body pressing against hers.

Cassidy almost said something along the lines of *I'm right here, you know,* as they talked across her, but the words wouldn't form and she realized they were still talking. She'd missed a bunch of it, and she was getting scared again, more scared than she had been. *Help,* Cassidy thought, and even the thought was too slow, too unformed. *Help. I don't want to die up here.*

She must have spoken aloud again. Cody pressed closer behind her and whispered in her ear, "Shh. Nobody's going to die. We'll keep each other warm." His cock stirred against her backside, rigid again, pressing between her cheeks.

Cassidy went still for an instant, then pushed back against Cody, moving her hips slightly. A small thrill of heat went through her. A second heartbeat started between her legs. She shifted slightly, pressed her upper body more tightly against Max's, feeling his body heat start up, and reached her hands down between them. Max was hard and thick and ready too.

The fire still burned, warm, but the flames had dropped. The light was gray, their faces indistinct as a dream.

No one spoke. There was no need. Each of them must have imagined some version of this at some time, Cassidy thought; she certainly had, whatever she'd led anyone else to believe. Now that she had her hands on Max's cock and was snuggled tight against Cody, everything seemed natural. Natural and right for Max to reach down and slide her top leg over his, to move his hips forward so the tip of his cock teased her clit, slid between her slick, wet lips, making her grind against him, Cody moving against her back. Cody's hand came around her body, playing with her breasts, pinching her nipples hard enough she could feel the blood flowing there fast. Her hands were tight around Max's shaft and he groaned, moved like a diver under the sleeping bag, coming up with his cock at her head level, feet unfortunately exposed but he didn't seem to care.

Cassidy flicked out her tongue, ran it the length of his rigid silkiness, teased him with a flurry of kitten licks before she sucked him hard into her mouth at the same time Max thrust hard into her, a muttered "Tease" before his mouth found her clit. No teasing there—he covered her clit with his mouth and started to suck.

Cassidy arched her back, felt Cody bite her shoulder and then position himself so he could slide inside of her.

Cassidy gasped at the size of his cock, giggled around Max's cock, was lightly bitten in reprimand, and then individual actions were unimportant, there was only shadowed movement, rhythmic rocking, sounds of pleasure, growing warmth. Max fucked her mouth and Cassidy used her tongue to tease and stroke him even as she sucked. Cody played with her nipples still, even as he rocked into her again and again and again and Cassidy rode his cock, glorying in the warmth inside her until that warmth burst wide open. She tightened up as she came, cunt and clit pulsing in rings of pleasure, triggering Cody to come, emptying himself into her. Her jaw tightened and Max left off sucking, said, "Ah, god," and filled her mouth with his come.

They lay together in a huddle, more arms and legs than seemed appropriate, and nobody wanted to move. But the fire needed tending and they needed to dig through their packs for water and energy bars and apples, which they ate under the sleeping bag, bodies pressed together. The food warmed her even more, and Cassidy shifted down between her best friends contentedly.

"What do you think you're doing?" Max asked.

Cassidy blinked at him and at Cody in case he knew what Max was talking about. Cody gave a little shrug and Cassidy realized none of them seemed very injured now. Apparently they had their minds on other things.

"Sleeping?" Cassidy asked. "There's not much to do." She would have gestured at the cave, the snow, the non-functioning cell phones, but it was warmer under the covers and she had no interest in moving.

"We have to keep warm," Max said, and Cassidy thought she heard something in his voice.

"I *am* warm," she said. "Aren't you?"

Cody gave a soft laugh. He sounded almost asleep.

"For now," Max said. Just for an instant the fire flared and

Cassidy got a look at his face. He looked mischievous. Anything but sleepy. "But we have to make sure we *stay* that way." He shifted under the bedroll and pressed himself against her thigh. He was hard again, hard as he had been earlier. Cassidy smiled in the dim fire-lit cave. "Cody? Are you warm enough?" She slid her free hand down to circle his cock, long, hard, very ready.

"I could be warmer," Cody said.

Sunlight woke them in the morning, along with the sound of birdsong and snow melting off the overhang to the cave. The fire was almost out, their clothes damp and unappealing, but the sun was shining and it seemed midsummer had returned.

We should make sure we're all warm enough before we have to leave, Cassidy thought as the men on either side of her began to stir. But from outside the cave came the sound of multiple pairs of hiking boots, voices loud in the quiet morning air.

"I think I see—yeah, it's a cave, hang on, back there, might not need it," and then, "Hey in there, anyone home?" and then a smiling search-and-rescue guy appeared at the cave entrance. "You folks okay? We thought we'd get you breakfast in bed and then take you down the mountain. How about it?"

The guy had very white teeth and ebony skin, a shaved head and a lot of muscles. Cassidy was suddenly very aware of the men on either side of her and the sleeping bag that was all there was between them and the search-and-rescue guy.

"An escort would rock," Cody said, the sleeping bag sliding to his waist. Their rescuer tried to look impassive. "Just give us a minute or two? We had wet clothes and were trying to share body heat last night."

Their rescuer nodded and gave them a grin that clearly meant *right, of course you were,* and ducked back out of the cave opening, standing with his back to them.

Cassidy could hear the voices of two or there more people outside the cave.

"Rise and shine," Max said. "Unless you'd prefer to stay here?" He pushed out from under the bag, naked and not at all embarrassed.

Cassidy didn't blush. Instead, she said, "Well, we could always invite him in to get warm before we go."

Max laughed. Cody was mock appalled.

Their clothes were clammy but not unmanageably so. Just before they shouldered their packs, Max said, "So I guess you're never going hiking again, huh, Cass?"

And she grinned at him. "I don't know," she said. "There's hiking, and then there's *hiking*." She licked her lips and laughed at their startled, hopeful faces.

"Besides, we didn't die up here."

UNCHARTED
SEAS

Chris Komodo

Sophia looked through the windows of the darkened helm, over the luxury yachts and out to the hotels and casino lighting up the night, before sinking back down onto the captain's chair and the man seated in it.

The glow from across the harbor outlined her lightly tanned breasts. Lower down, shadows fell across her long legs as they straddled her Italian race-car driver on the bridge of the *Grand Sultan.*

Sophia was in the driver's seat for the moment, but it wasn't her ship. She couldn't have afforded to charter the four-hundred-foot mega-yacht for a day, let alone for the eight months she and Eve were sailing. Their rig sat tied on the public side of the harbor, a modest thirty-five-foot catamaran two competent sailors could handle. A past owner had stenciled its name on the stern: *Wanderlust.*

Eve and Sophia had met at a sailing clinic organized by their Massachusetts university's alumni group. Both active and in their midthirties, they hit it off and spent occasional Saturdays sailing together off the shores of Cape Cod. Two years later, they both needed a break from the East Coast and the constant family pressures to find a husband. So they flew to Barcelona, chartered the catamaran and set sail on the Mediterranean Sea.

To pay for it they spent a few weeks at each port working. Eve, the more outgoing and spontaneous of the two, usually tended bar or waited tables. Her light hair and Scandinavian features brought her plenty of welcome interest from men.

The more career-minded Sophia, a graphic designer, worked from her laptop on board *Wanderlust*. Her captivating eyes, creamy skin and long legs attracted attention too, but her intelligence and nearly six feet of height limited the men who pursued her to the secure and confident ones. Which was fine with Sophia.

She fell for one of them on Sardinia. She and Luca had floated around the vineyards, coves and cafes of his home island together. She made drawings of the vines, the cliffs and the muscles of his back. The days and nights blurred together in a haze of beach sand, olive oil, and Grenache, of sex and passion, arousal and release.

Sophia had believed she was in love. But after the last round of heady, wet lovemaking on her last night on Sardinia, Luca had told Sophia he would come and find her after sunrise. The next morning, as they untied the last line from the last cleat, he was nowhere.

True to form, Eve had remarked, "Good! Screw love. Let's sail to Monaco!"

The two friends now gazed out across the water at the world-famous city of Monte Carlo, Monaco. The films didn't lie; the city teemed with fancy cars, lavish hotels, and extravagant yachts owned by Saudi princes and billionaire playboys.

Thanks to a connection back in Marseilles, Eve was working nights as a hostess on the *Grand Sultan*, one of the largest yachts in the harbor. But Sophia's days drawing corporate logos on *Wanderlust* were growing dull, and she'd seen little of the fine dining and glamorous lifestyle she'd heard so much about.

One night, while the two were washing dishes in the cramped galley of their boat, Eve suggested a diversion. "You could always come and help out on the *Sultan*. There's like, a dozen staff on food and drinks alone. One or two are usually no-shows; I could easily switch you in. No one would notice; all you'd have to do is serve drinks and look pretty."

"Sounds like a scene from a Bond film," Sophia replied. "I'm not sure I could pull off the whole undercover thing."

"Well, it would get you off this boat awhile and you could see what a Monte Carlo party is like," Eve offered. "At least come and see the yacht, Sophia, it's insane! I heard it has a ballroom and a swimming pool, and I haven't found either of them yet. Look, I have to head out soon, but if you feel like checking it out tonight try to come by before eight, when the guests start arriving. I'll tell the guard on the gangway to send you up my way."

After Eve left, Sophia went down to the berth below deck and lay back on the bed they shared, to lose herself in her romance novel. Her eye caught sight of some underthings Eve had laid out on the bedspread. Some lace, some silk, most of them black and all of them daring.

Eve must have been choosing which one to wear tonight. Did she have plans with a man after work? She ran the back of her fingers along the fabric of a pink pair. They were soft, light—and see-through. She felt a tinge of excitement, as if she had spied someone undressing through an open door.

Eve came by adventures easily, and Sophia envied her for it.

Eve would often come back late to the boat after a date—usually a guy she had met at work (but on two occasions, a woman). She would share the details with Sophia, who was always curious and—more than once—a little aroused.

Like the time in Mallorca when Eve had slept with the new bartender. She had come aboard still pretty tipsy and started recounting the night as she undressed. Sophia had watched from the bed as Eve wiggled out of her miniskirt. The two weren't shy about undressing in front of each other; bunking together on *Wanderlust* had instilled a certain intimacy between them. And while Sophia's interests had only ever involved men, she always enjoyed watching Eve's breasts—fuller and rounder than her own—pop out of her bra or bikini as she would unclasp it and toss it aside. That night, still a little drunk from the martinis, Eve stepped out of her black thong and collapsed onto the bed, not bothering to get under the sheets.

Her eyes closed, she had told Sophia how she had seduced the young bartender after their shift and walked with him to his apartment. She described how he had pressed her up against the wall as he kissed her and felt under her shirt, and how they'd never even made it to his bedroom: he had just pulled her panties aside in the entryway of his flat and fucked her standing up.

As Eve described it all, Sophia could see her squeezing her breast with one hand while the other rubbed in between her legs. Sophia listened closely while, under the covers, she silently stroked her own clit. Hearing Eve's explicit account while watching her play with herself had brought Sophia to a delicious, secret orgasm.

Growing drowsy as she finished her story, Eve turned on her side, her pillowy breast pressing against Sophia's arm, and kissed her on the cheek before lying back and falling asleep.

That was a month ago. Tonight Eve was out as usual, and

if Sophia stayed on board working she knew she'd go to bed lonely again. So she threw her book aside and headed for her wardrobe.

The sky over Monte Carlo had faded to a deep, dark blue when Sophia arrived at the private section of the harbor. Warm yellow cabin lights made the large yachts glow from the inside.

She found her way to the end of the dock and to the largest ship. The stern read, *Grand Sultan, Dubai.* She followed the guard's directions to the galley, eventually passing through the main lounge. The high ceilings, fine furniture and grand piano reminded her of a five-star hotel, but suggestive sculptures and a large circular couch made her think of sex.

She found Eve in the kitchen where staff were pulling champagne bottles out of cases and sticking toothpicks into appetizers. "Dang, Eve, I didn't know you were wearing *this* every night!"

Eve turned to see Sophia coming across the room. "Hey! Oh, the dress. All the girls are wearing this tonight."

It was black, sleek and short, and it hugged her figure tightly. The back wrapped around her neck like a choker. A small *Sultan* insignia sewn on the chest was the only reminder she was there to serve the guests.

"So are you passing out hors d'oeuvres or *entertaining?*" Sophia raised her eyebrows suggestively.

"Ha ha, Sophie. We don't dress this slutty for every event. But tonight the owner's hosting a party to welcome a bunch of Formula One racers to town—the Grand Prix starts in a few days. They're all guys, mostly young, so the dress code tonight is sexy. You should wander around and check the place out, but when everyone's here you'll need to bolt."

Sophia looked through the kitchen doors as the guests started arriving. Not that she knew any race-car drivers, even the famous ones. But her eyes fixed on one man strolling across the lounge. Was he one of the racers? He was a little older than the others. He sported a tuxedo, and damn well. It didn't look like a costume on him as it did on the younger guys.

He carried himself confidently, more suave than cocky, she thought. His hair was dark and handsomely styled, but a couple days' worth of facial hair added a bit of edge. He now stood casually by the piano with his hands in his pockets, laughing at something one of the other racers said.

Sophia turned and found Eve again and said brusquely, "I want to work tonight."

"Why the change of heart, Sophia? We're actually okay for help now, everyone showed up."

"No, let me help out, please."

"Ooh, I get it!" Eve pounced. "Something to do with the guests here tonight, huh? Someone's caught your eye and you want to see more, am I right?"

"Oh come on, Eve. Yes. Yes, okay? He's hot and...well, he seems mature, and..."

"Okay, okay, don't get defensive. I just wanted you to admit it, that's all." She touched her arm reassuringly. "I can get you on staff, I'll just say we miscounted. I have a pair of heels you can borrow, but you know you're going to have to wear one of these little numbers too, right?" Eve patted her dress.

Sophia nodded and grinned. Eve hurried her downstairs to the wardrobe.

Sophia removed her skirt, blouse and bra in front of the floor-to-ceiling mirror. Eve handed her one of the dresses from the rack and she stepped into it. Eve tied it off around her neck. "Well?" Sophia asked, eyeing her reflection.

"Umm, it fits in the bust and hips, but I don't think it was made for a girl as tall as you." Her dress fit even shorter than Eve's.

"It's perfect," she retorted.

"Ooh, I like this side of you!" Eve beamed, squeezing Sophia's hand.

They returned to the kitchen area, now bustling with activity. Eve grabbed one of the silver trays, pulled out Sophia's arm, and loaded her up with five glasses of Krug.

"Okay, double-oh-seven, keep your balance, don't talk too much, and keep the drinks flowing," Eve instructed. "Go get 'em. Or should I say, *him?*"

Sophia emerged from the swinging door and walked across the lounge. A sultry saxophone version of "Girl from Ipanema" played through the speakers and she scanned the room for her target. The space was buzzing with conversations in French and Italian. She spotted him talking in a circle with three other racers.

"Champagne?" Sophia offered. Hell, she figured, it's the same word in any language.

Masculine hands found their way to the glasses on her tray, but only one of the men looked at her directly. The light from a chandelier sparkled in his eyes, and she kept his gaze, displaying none of the submissiveness expected from waitstaff.

"Thank you, Miss...?"

"Sophia," she responded, gracefully, before wondering how he knew she spoke English. As she headed back for the kitchen she thought she could feel his eyes exploring her legs and ass.

Sophia found opportunities to get close to him several more times throughout the party. Eve had seen him before and told her he was Italian and that his name was Sergio. Sophia wanted to get to know him—actually, she wanted to do a lot more to him—but she tried to keep in character.

Later in the night, Sophia helped the remaining staff put

away empty bottles and load up dishwashers. Eve had disappeared, and when Sophia reemerged into the lounge the party had devolved into a smaller, looser affair. Some of the racers were smoking and playing poker at a round mahogany table. Most of the staff had left, but some of the younger hostesses stuck around, chatting or flirting with the guests.

Unable to find Sergio, Sophia left the lounge and headed outside into the warm Mediterranean air. She rested her arms against the handrail, looked to the twinkling casino and listened to the clanging of wire rope against distant masts. She thought back to Sardinia and reminded herself not to mistake passion for love again. "This isn't a husband-finding voyage," Eve had told her, "and you're not going to find love on a three-week port stop. Just live in the moment, Sophie."

A few yards down the walkway, one of the bartenders was leaning back on the railing, a hostess nuzzled up against his neck. Sophia felt the night air brushing against her exposed thighs. She watched the couple and longed for some attention of her own.

"What do you see?" an Italian voice asked over her shoulder. She turned around to see Sergio standing before her, as sharp and handsome as he was when he first strolled into the lounge. Was he referring to the view of Monte Carlo or of the couple down the way rubbing against each other?

"It's a lovely city," she replied. "It's a shame you're only here for the race."

"It is beautiful," he agreed, "but one can find beauty wherever one is."

His line echoed something Luca had said to her about beauty on Sardinia, thirty minutes before she had fucked him on a blanket between the rows of grapevines.

"I think I've read this story before," she retorted. "Isn't this when you offer to show me the view from the bridge and then somehow we end up in your cabin?"

Sergio only smiled, politely.

"You *are* staying on the ship tonight like the other guys, right?" she prodded.

"Yes, I have a cabin on board. It is, eh, adequate."

She was practically dangling sex in front of him. Maybe he wasn't like other men, who never passed up an opportunity to get laid.

Which only made her want him more. She had wanted every inch of him when she first spied him through the kitchen doors. But now she knew better than to plan beyond tonight.

Sergio gazed out at the hills above the city, focused and serene. He was thinking about his upcoming race. Or maybe a girlfriend or wife at home. Or maybe—

She didn't care. She wanted his eyes, his chiseled face, his calm self-confidence. She wanted him naked, under her.

"Sergio?" she took his hand and stepped closer to him. "Can we go to your cabin and get out of these clothes?"

His mouth grew a warm smile. "Nothing would please me more, Sophia."

She took his arm and they walked back through the lounge and up an elegant spiral staircase walled in glass. "They gave me the Sultan's Suite for the night, as team captain," Sergio explained, "but first, as you like, I will show you the view."

Three decks up, the pair emerged onto the *Sultan's* bridge. Ahead of them a ten-foot-wide dashboard of screens, controls and instruments lined the front wall of the helm. Windows on all sides offered a 360-degree view around the yacht, and the floors and paneling shined with clean, glossy wood. The bridge was dark but for the glow emanating from the displays and the lights from the casino falling in through the windows.

They walked to the side facing Monte Carlo. "The city is gorgeous," Sophia marveled, before turning to Sergio and pulling him closer. "Let's not go to your cabin," she said.

She tugged on his shirt, exposing his chest. Little tuxedo studs popped out and clanked down onto the wood flooring. She reached around to unclasp his cummerbund while he tossed his shirt on the dashboard, shrouding the green light of a monitor.

Grasping his waistband, she pulled him against her for a long, deep kiss, her tongue exploring his warm mouth. Her fingers lowered his zipper and his trousers dropped, revealing formfitting, navy-blue, Euro-style briefs. Sophia never cared for such underwear, but the bulge formed by his sizeable package set her heartbeat racing.

She tugged this final barrier down and his weighty cock sprang free. She savored the sight of it, not yet full but ample in girth.

Sophia looked around. She eyed the captain's chair, set atop a swivel post to give a commanding view around. She led Sergio over and sat him down in it, his body bare against the tan leather, cock swelling in anticipation of this bold American girl.

On the bridge of the *Grand Sultan* Sophia stood in a dress shorter than anything she'd ever worn back home. She felt as if anyone looking out of a hotel room beyond the dock could, with a decent pair of binoculars, make out her figure in the dim glow of lights. Sophia felt more alive in that moment than she had in years.

She turned around, her back facing Sergio, slid her hands up the sides of her legs, and hooked her thumbs over the waist of her panties. Swaying her ass slowly from side to side, she pulled them down beneath her dress, bit by bit, until they appeared around her thighs and she let them fall to the floor around her high heels. She stepped out of them, picked them up, smiled seductively and tossed them against the control panel, hooking them over a black dial.

She noticed the effect this had on his cock, now fully engorged, pointing straight up from his balls. "Please make me wait no more, Sophia," he urged.

"I have been waiting for this since I served you that first champagne, Sergio," she replied. She walked her fingers playfully up the inside of his leg toward his cock. Finally, she climbed onto his lap, facing him, her knees resting on the upholstery on either side of him. The position hiked Sophia's already short dress up even higher, and she felt the warm skin of his thighs against her bare bottom.

Her chest hovered at Sergio's eye level. Looking at the *Sultan* insignia he said, "You don't really work on this ship, do you, Sophia?"

"Was it that obvious?" she chuckled. She reached her hands behind her neck and untied the choker holding her dress up. The front panel fell away, baring her breasts to Sergio's gaze. She leaned forward and rested her forearms on the back of the chair, letting her soft breasts brush against his face. Sergio's mouth found one of her nipples and encircled it with his lips, lapping at the tip with playful swirls of his tongue.

As Sophia closed her eyes to savor the pleasure she heard the rising sound of heels on hardwood. Before she could think what to do, a woman appeared at the top of the stairs and stopped in her tracks. She saw Sophia's top half over the back of the captain's chair, and noticed a man's dress shirt and woman's panties strewn across the helm.

"Whoa, there you are, Sophie." It was Eve. "Sorry, I didn't mean to interrupt anything."

"Oh, no worries," Sophia replied playfully. "Sergio here was just showing me the helm." She looked down at him. "Weren't you, Serge?"

"I was going to see if you were ready to walk back with me,

but I see you're...occupied." Eve was smiling wickedly. "You know, if you weren't interested in Sergio I would have gone for him myself. I like your taste, Sophie. Well, I'll leave you two alone then. I'll wait for you down in the lounge." She turned to descend the stairway.

"Hold on," Sophia called after her.

She turned back around. "Yeah?"

"Why don't you wait"—Sophia paused to gather her nerve— "with us, up here?"

Eve considered it for a moment. "Oh, that's kinky, Sophie." She bounded back up the last two stairs and plunked herself down on one of the padded benches along the side wall.

Sophia had never been watched before. Eve was her friend, but she couldn't deny a certain fascination with her body and her ease and experience with sex. They had shared a lot with each other in the last months, and sharing this now felt comfortable and natural. Not to mention exciting.

As Sergio's lips returned to Sophia's breasts, Eve kicked off her heels, leaned back against the cushion and placed her bare feet on the seat near her ass so she had a view of the action between her bended knees. She moved her hand straight to her pussy and started stroking it through her panties. With a profile view of the couple, she could see Sophia's breasts and erect nipples, and brief glimpses of the racer's rigid cock.

Sophia reached down to grasp it and stroked it while Sergio continued to suck on her breasts. She felt soaked between her legs and positioned herself so her pussy hovered just over his bulbous cockhead. Spreading her legs wider, she lowered herself just an inch more so that her lips captured and cradled the tip of his cock near her warm entrance.

She turned her head sideways to see Eve rubbing herself with firm, swift strokes. But rather than watching Sergio, Eve's focus pointed squarely on Sophia.

As she teased the waiting cock beneath her, Sophia's gaze stayed locked on Eve's. So deep was the girls' familiarity with each other by now that Sophia could read Eve's ecstasy in the subtle softening of her eyelids, while Eve could recognize Sophia's bliss in her slowly rising cheek muscles.

"Come over here," Sophia said softly, beckoning Eve closer.

Eve slid off the seat and walked across the bridge toward the captain's chair. Sophia grasped her hands and continued to look into her eyes, just inches now from her own.

A mischievous look crossed Sophia's face and in the next instant she lowered herself down onto Sergio. She lost focus on Eve as she took his full length all at once, her head falling back and her mouth opening wide as she felt him fill her completely.

Eve looked on with wide eyes. When Sophia regained her bearings she looked back to her and they shared a laugh. But the levity soon passed as Sophia's attention returned to Sergio's cock, which he had started working in and out of her. Her hips began rocking rhythmically, instinctively.

Sergio took control now, holding her by the hips as he drove himself inside her with strong, repeated thrusts. As Sergio's pounding intensified, Sophia squeezed Eve's hands and pulled her even closer.

Eve gazed back on Sophia's flushed cheeks and closed the remaining distance, pressing her mouth against her friend's. In Sophia's lips she felt the energy of her excitement and the echoes of each of the racer's thrusts driving into her.

As Sophia felt an orgasm nearing, Eve broke their kiss to put her mouth by Sophia's ear and whisper, "I want to watch you come, Sophie."

The words pushed Sophia over the edge. Eve placed her cheek against Sophia's and ran her hand through her hair as she came, cradling the back of her head as she cried out from the growing waves of pleasure. Sergio's raw fucking and Eve's tender caresses combined to overwhelm Sophia's senses, leaving her dizzy and euphoric long after her orgasm subsided.

By the next weekend, the girls had cast off from the Monte Carlo harbor and were once again plying the blue waters of the Mediterranean. They didn't leave, though, before sharing one more tryst with the Italian racer, this time on board *Wanderlust* and with Eve's complete involvement.

Now on their way to Naples, Sophia lay back on the deck under the warm sun while watching Eve steer and reflecting on their journey, in its final weeks.

Sergio, of course, was only a fling, but one she'd sorely needed. As for Eve...her feelings for Eve weren't purely sexual, though desire was part of it. And they weren't exactly romantic love, though there was love too.

They were exploring new waters somewhere beyond the familiar seas of friendship. Sophia had sacrificed ease and certainty, but in return, gained a deep, soul-filling sense of contentment. And that, for now, was everything.

THREE FOR
THE ROAD

Kristina Wright

It had seemed liked a good idea, in theory. But as with most theories, I wasn't entirely sure it would work. Either something magical would happen or it would be a disaster, there didn't seem to be any other option and, in my panicky mind as we loaded the car and climbed in, there didn't seem to be any gray area, either.

When I'd suggested a vacation, first with my husband, Joe, and then with my boyfriend, Eric, I had meant separately. But in looking over the finances, and my increasingly busy work schedule, it had seemed unlikely I could manage two vacations. And so, after a few Friday night happy hour drinks, I'd suggested the three of us go together. Joe and Eric liked each other, had known each other for five years and been happy (usually) being in dual relationships with me for nearly as long.

I'm not sure how it started, this strange and wonderful life of mine, except that Joe always knew I was a free spirit. He knew I was attracted to Eric before I did, I think, and when the opportunity arose for me to explore that avenue, he'd encouraged it. He said he was secure in our relationship and would never stop me from exploring my interests, whatever they were. What's not to love about a guy like that? Eric, newly divorced and exploring his own interests, had been happy to go to bed with me once he knew everything was out in the open with my spouse, and then had fallen in love with me. Maybe I loved him, too; I wasn't sure, but I did my best to balance my feelings and affections accordingly. There were no secrets, no lies and only occasional jealousies, which were rarely about sex and only occasionally about emotions. Most often, conflicts were over what precious free time I had—or over seeing a movie with one that the other one wanted to see.

I ran all these thoughts through my head as I piled the last of my stuff in the back of the Jeep. The guys were amiably strapping the cargo carrier on top, which held our tent—ours, as in all three of us sleeping in one tent—and sleeping bags. I had suggested camping in Asheville as a cheap alternative to a resort stay, but that was when it had been just Joe and me. Now I was wishing I'd opted for the resort. At least there would've been a king-sized bed and a pullout sofa, just in case things got weird. But I seemed to be the only one concerned.

"I GPS'd it and it's about a six-hour drive to the campsite," Joe said. "How about we do a three-way split?"

Threeway? Did he really have to say it like that?

"That's cool." Eric was putting air in his bicycle tires. "Let me just get the bikes mounted, and I'll be ready."

Threeway? Mounted? Were they deliberately torturing me or was it just my dirty mind wondering how three nights in a tent—already cramped with two people—was going to go? They both seemed oblivious to my discomfort.

"Count me out," I said, sounding even more surly than normal at six a.m. "I need a nap."

With that pronouncement, I climbed into the backseat, adjusted my pillow and feigned drowsiness as they finished the last packing details and got into the front seat. There, that put my mind at ease. Taking turns sitting next to them while we headed off into the woods and whatever three-way debauchery we could get into would only make me hyperventilate. Because, despite this very nontraditional, and generally awesome, arrangement I have, I'd never actually had a threesome. Oh sure, I'd talked about it—with both of them. But again, it was only a theory, one of those late-night chats designed to fan the flames and ramp up the sex. A kind of "what if" game where the men, who were both voyeurs, each imagined me with the other. Of course, neither of them seemed to consider the complication of being able to watch because *they were also in the bed,* and neither seemed bothered by the logistics of such a fantasy. It was all fun and games until two vacations merged into one.

"You okay back there, Desi?" Joe asked as he hit the interstate. "You're awfully quiet."

"She's resting up," Eric said, and they both laughed.

"I'm sleeping," I muttered, and turned my head into my pillow. Damn them. Why did I care how this weekend went? Really? It was on them, not on me. Right?

Of course I knew that wasn't true. I didn't want to risk either relationship over a botched threeway. I didn't want anyone's feelings to get hurt. I sure as hell didn't want to feel like I had to perform some sort of porn-movie-inspired act of the girl in the middle. But what was done was done, or soon to be done, I mused. Might as well go with the flow and see what happened.

I really did fall asleep at some point and missed the driver switch. I woke up with an urgent need to pee and a crick in my neck. I started to tell them they needed to pull over, but then I heard my name.

"...told Desi it would be okay, but now I'm starting to freak out," Joe said from the passenger seat. "What if it doesn't work out?"

"Hey, man, I have no experience in it, but if anyone can figure it out, you can."

Well, that was awfully selfish of Eric, putting it all on Joe.

"Thanks. I think so. I just want to be good at it, you know? Do it right the first time."

"You will," Eric reassured him. "And then she'll want to do it again."

I was about ready to scream. Now it was Joe who felt the pressure to perform?

"What about you? Ever considered it?"

Eric sighed. "Not really my thing. My ex wasn't interested and I really think I'm too selfish to make it work."

"Yeah? That's not what Desi says. She thinks you'd be great, said you have the skill set for it."

"I guess we'll see," Eric said noncommittally. "But it's nice to know she thinks so."

What the...? I had *never*, never talked to Joe about Eric's prowess in bed. It was my own personal honor code not to discuss the nitty-gritty about one with the other one. I was boiling angry at this point, at both of them.

"I have to go to the bathroom," I announced loudly, not caring if they knew I'd overheard them or not.

"We're almost to the campsite." Joe didn't sound perturbed at all. "Be there in a few, and you can hit the head while we set up the tent."

Just like that. No big deal that they'd been talking about our

impending threesome a minute ago. I didn't know why it bothered me. It just did.

The campsite was empty except for one other tent at the far side.
It was late in the season. Summer was over and the evenings
were turning cool. The idea that the three of us would be practically alone for the weekend should've been exciting, but I just
couldn't shake this bad mood. The guys put up the tent while I
stomped off to the communal bathroom and shower. It would
serve them right, I mused, if I just said no to sex all weekend.
Then what would they do?

It wasn't likely, though. My sex drive had always been off the
charts and even angry I was likely to jump either one of them if
the occasion arose. The only answer was to clear the air. I got
back to our campsite and helped them finish unloading the Jeep.
By the time we were done, it was growing dark. Eric was busy
building a campfire when I nudged Joe.

"I need to talk to you. Privately."

The guys exchanged a look and Joe shrugged. "Okay."

I expected him to walk away from the campfire, but instead
he ducked into the tent. I let out a sigh and followed him.

"This is hardly private," I mumbled, flopping down on our
scrunched-together sleeping bags. "He can hear every word."

"No I can't," Eric called.

"What's up?"

I stared at Joe. "Seriously? You want to do this here?"

"I didn't want to do anything. You did. You've been acting
strange since we left, but this was your idea. So what's up?"

He said it gently, almost with some sense of understanding
of how I was feeling, which wasn't surprising. Joe knew me
better than anyone, and Eric was a close second. So what was
up with me?

I shook my head. "Nerves, I guess. Just nerves. Sorry."

He nodded. "That's what I figured. There's nothing to be nervous about, though. It's supposed to be fun. If it works, great. If not, we're all still friends and everything stays the same."

"You didn't sound so confident in the Jeep," I muttered, but I nodded. "Okay. You're right."

"Confident?" A look of realization crossed his face. "Oh— you heard us."

I nodded, half launching myself into his lap before another case of nerves took over. "It doesn't matter. What you just said makes complete sense. Nothing changes because of this weekend. It's supposed to be fun. It *will* be fun."

He started to speak, but I kissed him. This was my comfort zone, kissing Joe. Sitting on Joe's lap in our cozy tent, making out and feeling his erection swell under my bottom. This was what I wanted. Needed. We kissed for several long minutes, his arms around me, the sound of the fire crackling outside the tent.

Outside the tent. I remembered Eric.

"Would you like to join us?" I called, knowing he had to realize what was going on inside the tent.

The tent flat opened and he pushed past Joe's broad shoulders. "I thought you'd never ask. I was just going to make a postcoital dinner for the two of you and hope for the best in the morning."

We all laughed at that and I remembered what had attracted me to Eric in the first place—he had a way of soothing me with humor, putting things in perspective. I had no doubt that he would, in fact, have stayed outside and made dinner no matter what Joe and I did in the tent. He wouldn't get angry, he wouldn't pressure me. He'd wait until I was ready for whatever and then he'd be up for it. So would Joe. And I hadn't had to coerce either

of them here. This was a group decision, a three-way choice. My
guys and me.

I started unbuttoning my flannel shirt while Joe nibbled at
my neck. I felt Eric's hands on my shoulders, kneading the tense
muscles there. He had great hands, as soothing as his voice.
With my shirt unbuttoned, I melted into Joe and Eric pulled my
shirt off. Without my telling him, he released the clasp of my
bra and pulled it from between Joe and me. Now I was topless
against Joe, who was rock hard and devouring the upper swell
of my breasts with his lips and tongue. It was the most basic
of foreplay, but Eric's presence made it as sexy as if we were
already going at it. The dull throb between my legs made me
anxious to get the rest of my clothes off. Whatever hesitations
and doubts I'd had before were gone now. Joe's familiar smell
mingled with Eric's for an intoxicating combination that had
me creaming my panties.

I shifted off Joe and practically fell into Eric's arms. "Help
me with my jeans?"

"Yes, ma'am," he said, the zipper loud in the quiet tent.

I got my boots off, then wiggled out of my jeans and
panties, conscious of both of them watching me. Silent, stoic,
unmoving—but I could feel the sexual tension like a presence,
rubbing against my naked skin the same way Eric was rubbing
my thigh and Joe was stroking my breast.

"Your turn," I said, not specifying which.

Slowly, they undressed on either side of me. I'd thought this
part would be weird, as neither of them had shown any bisexual
interests, but it seemed like the most natural thing in the world.
After some maneuvering to accommodate their long legs, they
were as naked as I was and our skin rubbed in interesting ways
that only fueled my desire.

I climbed on Joe's lap again, anxious to make sure my

husband knew he came first, always. He settled his hands on my waist as I lowered myself on him. I reached down to guide his cock into me, wetter than I think I've ever been. The sound of him sliding into my wetness was erotic as hell and Eric must have thought so, too, because I heard his groan, as if it was his cock instead of Joe's.

Joe raised and lowered me slowly on his cock, letting me get him good and wet, letting Eric see exactly what was going on. Eric stroked me from my neck to my waist and then lower, his hands warm on my ass as he cupped my cheeks in his large hands, squeezing and kneading and even raising and lowering me on Joe's cock. It was the most erotic sensation I had ever felt.

Then he moved behind me, kneeling between Joe's splayed legs, his cock pressed firmly to the crack in my ass. I tensed, having never really considered double-penetration outside of having seen it in porn. I didn't think I could manage it. Wasn't even sure I wanted to try.

As if reading my mind, Eric pulled my hair back and whispered in my ear, "Relax, babe. We're not going there now. I just want to feel you."

That was good enough for me. I leaned back into Eric's arms, enjoying the support of his chest and the press of his cock while Joe thrust up into me, his gaze between my legs where his cock went into me. What had seemed erotic before was now just a prelude to this.

"Ohh," I moaned softly as Eric reached around to cup my breasts while Joe fucked me. He kissed and nibbled my neck and I could see Joe looking from our joined bodies to Eric's face.

"This is nice," I whispered when he finally looked at me.

His smile was devastating. "Just wait."

I didn't know what he meant until he raised me up and pulled his cock free, leaving me feeling empty. I started to pout, but as if they had choreographed it, Eric pushed me forward over Joe and slid into me from behind. It was a strange sensation, but not at all unwelcome. I knew their bodies so well, but though they had similar builds they felt different, fucked different. I was just adjusting to Eric's steady pounding rhythm when he slid out of me and pulled me back for Joe to enter me again. Back and forth they went for a few long strokes each, like the world's kinkiest seesaw and I was the fulcrum that held them together.

The differences in position and rhythm were making for a slow climb to orgasm for all of us. At some point, I couldn't take it anymore.

"One at a time," I gasped, riding Joe's cock hard. "I need to come."

Joe pushed me back against Eric's chest. "Whatever you want, sweetheart."

Eric reached around and found my clit, strumming it lightly while he was grinding his cock against my ass. Joe gripped my hips in his hands and slammed me down on his cock, fucking me hard and deep, just the way I needed. It was moments before I was coming, crying out as the dual sensations drove me into oblivion. My tightening pussy worked along Joe's overstimulated cock and he was right there with me in moments, nearly bucking me off him as he added his groans to my cries.

I fell forward across Joe's chest, feeling like I'd been ripped apart from the inside out and would never be the same again. It dawned on me that Eric was resting his body across mine, supporting his weight on his knees and hands so as not to crush Joe beneath us. I didn't feel the weight of his erection against my ass and realized from the wetness I could feel trickling down my lower back that he must have come at some point. I almost felt bad for being oblivious to his pleasure, but after a moment he started to laugh.

"That was the sexiest thing I've ever seen, done or felt."

Joe grunted in agreement.

"Sorry you didn't exactly get the best ending," I muttered.

"Next time," he said.

A shudder went through me. Next time. There was a promise in those words that I liked. But then I remembered I was still a little annoyed with both of them.

"But just for the record, I don't appreciate you guys talking about the sexy stuff while I'm sleeping."

"Huh?" Joe sounded like he was halfway to sleep.

"We have never talked about sex," Eric said.

"Yes you did, on the way here. I heard you. I never told Joe about your skills." I nipped Joe's shoulder hard enough to make him yelp. "And I don't care if you were feeling nervous, there was no reason to lie about it."

There was silence for a moment, then both men started to laugh. It was like being caught between two waves, their bodies rippling with me in between.

"What the hell is so funny?" They were seriously messing with my peaceful mood. "Just because it worked out doesn't mean you get to laugh at me."

"Sweetheart," Joe said, cupping my hand in his face. "We weren't talking about sex. We were talking about being parents. You told me Eric would make a good father."

"He would," I said, realization dawning. "You were—"

"I was saying that we were thinking about having a baby and I was hoping I'd be a good parent," Joe finished.

Eric rolled off of me and collapsed on a sleeping bag. "You'd both be good parents."

"So would you," I said.

He shrugged, seeming more uncomfortable than he had through our entire sexual adventure. "Maybe someday."

This wasn't exactly the pillow talk I was expecting, but it kind of hit me that this little trip was a good test to see if the three of us could live together. I couldn't imagine life without Eric, but I also couldn't imagine not starting a family in a few years. I shifted off of Joe, sandwiching myself between them. He was smiling enigmatically, as if he realized I was going through the same through process he had.

"Maybe with us," I said slowly, looking to Joe for agreement. He nodded slowly, and I released a breath I hadn't known I was holding.

Eric slipped his arm around my waist, snuggling against my hip. I mimicked his move, flinging a leg over Joe. I had never felt so safe or so loved in all my life.

"Maybe that would work," Eric said. "But not this weekend, okay?"

Joe laughed. "Not this weekend."

I was in agreement, but now they both had me thinking. Could we do it? Was it possible? I idly stroked Joe back to erection while Eric watched, his cock rising hard and insistent to press against my hip until I took him in my other hand. I looked from one to the other, watching their expressions as I stroked them, feeling myself growing aroused, as well. It didn't seem strange to be with both of them this way.

Anything was possible, I decided as I rolled over and straddled Eric. Anything at all.

ABOUT THE
AUTHORS

Over the past ten years, **CHEYENNE BLUE's** erotica has appeared in over seventy erotic anthologies and on numerous websites. Visit her website at cheyenneblue.com.

RACHEL KRAMER BUSSEL (rachelkrammerbussel.com) has edited over fifty anthologies, including *Gotta Have It, The Big Book of Orgasms, Baby Got Back: Anal Erotica, Serving Him, Anything for You, Spanked, Cheeky Spanking Stories, Orgasmic, Do Not Disturb: Hotel Sex Stories, The Mile High Club, Fast Girls* and the *Best Bondage Erotica* series.

ANGELA CAPERTON (blog.angelacapteron.com) writes eclectic erotica that challenges genre conventions. Look for her stories published with Black Lace and eBury Publishing, Cleis, Circlet, Coming Together, eXtasy Books, HarperCollins Mischief, Renaissance Books and Side Real Press.

ARIEL GRAHAM lived briefly in Oregon, though she never climbed (or got lost on) Mount Hood. Today she shares her Northern Nevada home with her husband, a band of cats, and unseen nighttime visitors like bobcats and coyotes who pass through her rural backyard. Her work has appeared in previous Cleis Press anthologies such as *Serving Him*; *Best Lesbian Romance*; *Please, Sir* and *Please, Ma'am*.

SKYLAR KADE (skylarkade.com) writes erotic romance, usually of the kinky persuasion. She lives in California and spends her time asking the cabana boys to bring her more mimosas and feed her strawberries while she dreams up her next naughty adventure.

CHRIS KOMODO is a California-based writer. He expanded into erotica in 2012 with "The Maestra," the account of a shy but cunning wife and conductor. His latest story appears in *The Big Book of Orgasms*, published by Cleis Press.

AXA LEE is an erotica-writing Michigan farm girl, who grazes cattle in her yard and herds incorrigible poultry with a cowardly dog. She's written since her grandmother had to spell words for her. Her work appears in the anthologies *Shameless Behavior* and *Dirty Little Numbers*.

ANNABETH LEONG (annabethleong.blogspot.com) is good at nostalgia but poor at recalling specific dates. Ellora's Cave recently published her erotic-romance thriller *The Fugitive's Sexy Brother*. Her short erotica can be found in the Cleis Press anthologies *xoxo*, *Passion*, *Girl Crush* and more. She lives in Providence.

A. J. LYLE has had her short erotic stories published in anthologies with Xcite Books and Cleis Press. She began writing erotica a few years ago when a friend dared her to make a romance story spicy, and she has never gone back to just romance since.

JADE MELISANDE (KinkandPoly.com) is a sex, kink and relationship blogger and erotica writer living in the Midwest with her two partners. She has been published in numerous anthologies including *Spankalicious, Show Me, Serving Him, Cheeky Spanking Stories, Voyeur Eyes Only, Orgasmic, Lesbian Lust* and *Power Play.*

MINA MURRAY (minamurray.wordpress.com) is an Antipodean and whisky aficionado. Her work appears in Cleis Press and HarperCollins Mischief anthologies, including *Dressed to Impress, Lords and Ladies, Brief Encounters, Sudden Sex, Mammoth Book of Quick & Dirty Erotica, Baby Got Back* and *The Big Book of Orgasms.*

TIFFANY REISZ lives in Lexington, Kentucky, where she can often be found making up dirty bedtime stories and annoying her cats and boyfriend when she should be cleaning the bathroom. She is the author of *The Original Sinners* series from MIRA Books.

GISELLE RENARDE is a queer Canadian, avid volunteer, contributor to more than one hundred short-story anthologies, and author of books like *Anonymous, The Red Satin Collection* and *My Mistress' Thighs.* Ms. Renarde lives across from a park with two bilingual cats who sleep on her head.

KATHLEEN TUDOR is a rockin' erotic author and super-editor, with stories in anthologies from Cleis, Circlet, Storm Moon, HarperCollins Mischief, Circlet, Xcite and more. Check her out in *Best Bondage Erotica 2014* and online at Kathleen-Tudor.com.

ALISON TYLER (alisontyler.blogspot.com), the "Trollop with a Laptop," has written twenty-five erotic novels and edited more than sixty erotic anthologies including *Twisted*, *Torn* and *Smart Ass*. In all things important, she remains faithful to her partner of eighteen years, but she still can't choose just one perfume.

VERONICA WILDE (veronicawilde.com) is an erotic romance author whose work has been published by Cleis Press, Xcite Books, Bella Books, Liquid Silver Books and Samhain Publishing.

ABOUT
THE EDITOR

Described by The Romance Reader as "a budding force to be reckoned with," **KRISTINA WRIGHT** (kristinawright.com) is the editor of over fifteen published and forthcoming Cleis Press anthologies, including the best-selling *Fairy Tale Lust: Erotic Fantasies for Women*. Other titles include: *Dream Lover: Paranormal Tales of Erotic Romance*; *Steamlust: Steampunk Erotic Romance*; *Lustfully Ever After: Fairy Tale Erotic Romance*; *Duty and Desire: Military Erotic Romance*; *XOXO: Sweet and Sexy Romance; A Princess Bound: Naughty Fairy Tales for Women* and the *Best Erotic Romance* series. She is also the author/editor of the cross-genre book *Bedded Bliss: A Couple's Guide to Lust Ever After* for Cleis Press and the author of the erotic romance *Seduce Me Tonight* for HarperCollins Mischief. Her fiction has been published in over one hundred anthologies and her articles, interviews and book reviews have appeared in numerous publications, both print and online. She received the Golden Heart Award for Romantic Suspense from Romance

Writers of America for her first novel *Dangerous Curves* and she is a member of RWA as well as the special interest chapters Passionate Ink and Fantasy, Futuristic and Paranormal. She holds degrees in English and humanities and has taught composition and world mythology at the college level. Originally from South Florida, Kristina is living happily ever after in Virginia with her husband, Jay, and their two little boys.